Praise for *Queen of Sheba*

One of history's most intriguing characters, several cultures claim the mysterious Queen of Sheba as their own. This delightful rendition of the Queen's relationship with King Solomon piqued my curiosity and gave me an enchanting glimpse into this wealthy, powerful, legendary woman.

—Wendy K. Walters
Author of *Marketing Your Mind* and *Intentionality*

The mysterious person of the Queen of Sheba is brought alive in this book. Her search for peace, meaning, and love will strike a chord in every reader's heart.

—Rodney Kingstone
International Speaker and Author

Mattie Hon has masterfully crafted a historical fiction highlighting the treasures hidden within the story of the Queen of Sheba. She creatively blends fact and legend into a transformational work of literary art.

—Lance and Annabelle Wallnau
Lance Wallnau,
Founder and President of Lance Learning Group
Annabelle Wallnau,
Vice-President of Lance Learning Group

QUEEN of SHEBA

Blessings on
your journey!
Mattie Hon

The Half Has Never Been Told

QUEEN
of
SHEBA

MATTIE M. HON

TATE PUBLISHING
AND ENTERPRISES, LLC

Queen of Sheba
Copyright © 2015 by Mattie M. Hon. All rights reserved.
Library of Congress Control Number: 2015933192

No part of this publication may be reproduced, stored in a retrieval system or transmitted in any way by any means, electronic, mechanical, photocopy, recording or otherwise without the prior permission of the author except as provided by USA copyright law.

Scripture quotations marked (NKJV) are taken from the *New King James Version*. Copyright © 1982 by Thomas Nelson, Inc. Used by permission. All rights reserved.

This novel is a work of fiction. However, several names, descriptions, entities, and incidents included in the story are based on the lives of real people.

The opinions expressed by the author are not necessarily those of Tate Publishing, LLC.

Published by Tate Publishing & Enterprises, LLC
127 E. Trade Center Terrace | Mustang, Oklahoma 73064 USA
1.888.361.9473 | www.tatepublishing.com

Tate Publishing is committed to excellence in the publishing industry. The company reflects the philosophy established by the founders, based on Psalm 68:11,
"The Lord gave the word and great was the company of those who published it."

Book design copyright © 2015 by Tate Publishing, LLC. All rights reserved.
Cover design by Jim Villaflores
Interior design by Jake Muelle
Cover Image by ©Paul Matthew, www.fotosearch.com (for illustrative purposes only)

Published in the United States of America

ISBN: 978-1-63306-735-6
Fiction / Christian / Historical
15.03.12

I dedicate this book to my husband and children. Thank you for the abundant joy and laughter you add to my life. May future generations of our family find delight in this story.

Acknowledgments

I am forever grateful to all who helped make this book a reality. Many thanks to those who have prayed, encouraged, proofed, edited, and assisted me in the myriad of details that need to be completed to write a book. Special thanks to my Heavenly Father for entrusting me with this assignment and providing all that I needed to accomplish it.

Introduction

Many have found themselves allured by the mysterious story of the Queen of Sheba. The intrigue surrounding this woman has been a driving force behind assorted works of art, music, inspirational writings, fables, archaeological studies, and household legends. Her story is recorded in the religious writings of Christians, Jews, and Muslims. She is honored by the words of Jesus through quite shocking and extraordinary depiction.

People of the nations both East and West proudly identify the Queen of Sheba as part of their heritage. Ethiopian, Arab, African, and Egyptian historians are among the many who have written about her impact upon their countries.

Historical accounts usually do not give her a name, only identifying her as the queen of the country, Sheba, also known as Saba in ancient writings. Sheba means "host of heaven and peace." Arab writers, however, call her Queen Balkis and Ethiopians name her Makeda. Jesus referred to her as "the queen of the south." The ancient historian Josephus named her Nikaulis, queen of Ethiopia and Egypt.

Ethiopian legend suggests that she was born in 1020 BC. Some archaeologists and historians today believe evidence indicates that Sheba's borders once encompassed parts of present-day southern Arabia, Ethiopia, and possibly Egypt. During the period of history in which she lived, rulers were primarily identified by the territories over which they reigned. In keeping with that tradition, throughout this book, she will be addressed as the Queen of Sheba.

I, for one, am among those drawn into the story of this astonishing woman and have been profoundly inspired by her quest for wisdom. May the pages of this book transport you into rich wells of discovery that could impact your life forever.

1

Terror fills my heart as I frantically run through an endless maze of ghostly figures. Taunting words from vindictive voices shout at every turn. Frighteningly familiar, the tormenting messages condemn and criticize as though assigned to crush me. I am longing for sweet empowerment; instead, bitter arrows pierce me, threatening to destroy all of my strength.

The shadows of those long gone have no power to deliver me from harm. Poisoned words wrap themselves around me like an evil vine, hurling my battered frame from the pinnacle of doom into the ocean below. Oppression weighs me down like a thrust anchor, pressing me against the deep dark ocean bottoms, intent on forcing my life from me.

The faraway silhouette of my mother helplessly watches as my sense of value weakens beneath this negative cloak. "Father, where are you? I need your protection. I am as an invisible phantom, lost and out of reach from your affections. Please nurture me! Please rescue me! Please hold me in your arms and warm me by your loving glance. Be the stability of my inward places. I need you." My being cries out as though you were still present to hear me.

I struggle to break away from this raging war and fight toward the water's surface where I can breathe again and hope to recover from these strange enemies. The anguish, the darkness, the battle to escape…the bleakness of the ocean pit creates a sense of complete emptiness. "Let me breathe! Please let me breathe," I screamed within as I gasped for air.

"Queen, wake up," she heard as she felt a gentle touch upon her shoulder. "You have cried out again, my lady. As you slept, a cry was heard throughout the corridor. Here, sip the healing teas of Sheba. I have added oil of frankincense and honey to calm and steady you for the day."

When the Queen heard the soft voice of Abigail and roused herself, she realized that her body was engulfed in weary sweat from the tumultuous night. What a contrast there was between the cruel torment of her dreams and the sweet touch of her beloved attendant's hand. How comforting a kind gesture could feel after waking up in such distress.

Abigail's tender words helped navigate her from the stormy darkness into what would be another day spent in searching. Truly, she was seeking for wisdom to best lead her people, her country, and even for that which would satisfy the longings of her own soul. How she wished she knew someone who could help her discover the answers that she sought.

It would be difficult for the citizens of Marib, the capital of Sheba, to believe their Queen could be afflicted with such intense emotions and unrest. This would be impossible for them to imagine. She was seen as one who ruled with great dignity and who had been given unparalleled privilege in the lives they shared.

The Queen stood alone as a female monarch in her day. This inherited status made her conflicted soul seem even more perplexing, only adding to the unusual details of her journey as the Queen of Sheba. No one knew better than she that the very vulnerabilities of her nature, the weak injured places of her heart, were the motivation behind her desire to be kind and generous to the loyal subjects of her kingdom.

The Queen was thankful that she possessed an ability to intuitively see deeply into the hearts and emotions of those she served. She could not help it. She perceived and easily connected with what they felt. Perhaps the fact that she had known pain and trouble is what drove her to find ways to alleviate unnecessary suffering from her people. That one motivation exploded into hundreds of questions which insisted on finding answers. She wanted to secure a good future, a bright destiny for the people of Sheba.

So began another typical day for the one known as Queen of Sheba. It did not seem fitting that the head of a powerful nation would be given to such introspection. Many contemplations once again engaged her as she rose from her bed to begin her queenly duties.

The Queen often wondered why she sought answers for her people who were more prosperous than most. Sometimes, she felt detached from the reality that she was a Queen. Though she dutifully fulfilled her obligations, at times the journey within seemed more real than the outward one. Perhaps, the two would merge and one day explode into a unique gateway for her people. She ached for the realization of great purpose and destiny for her country, yearning for something beyond, something greater, something unexpected, though she could not envision what that would be.

2

"How wonderful! This gown fits the way I hoped it would," spoke the Queen. "Abigail, can you sculpt my hair as elegantly as you did for the last banquet? It was very exquisite!"

"Of course, my lady. I'll have you at your best for the meeting with your merchant lords this morning."

The Queen once again was refreshed by the pleasant voice of her faithful handmaiden. Abigail had been with her for many years and was selfless in her devotion. Indeed, they were close friends. Without words, they understood the inward workings of each other. Abigail's mother attended the Queen's mother. Her life in the palace gave her the distinction of understanding this monarch in ways that would never be known by others.

As Abigail pressed the last lock of hair into place, she could not help noticing the Queen's reflection in the palace pools. She was intrigued by Her Majesty's appearance. Even though the Queen was only in her midtwenties, her dark eyes reflected layers of great depth. She was a thinker, accustomed to assessing and drawing in observations, which she pondered in her heart. There was both authority and compassion unveiled in her glances. The prominence of her nose was the perfect measure to add to the regal look of a queen. Abigail had braided her dark locks of hair and, like an artist, carefully sculpted them along the sides of the jeweled crown.

Abigail loved seeing the Queen in her casual attire, not yet adorned with the splendor of gowns and exquisite robes. It was times like this that Abigail thought her beloved Queen was the most beautiful. Her skin was smooth as glass yet soft as silk. There was an iridescence about her face like the wings of a dragonfly illuminated with olive undertones. Her lips were naturally colored with shades of coral pink. Dark eyebrows framed her large slightly almond-shaped eyes, giving her the distinctive look of soft sophistication unspoiled by arrogance.

The Queen held no guile, but displayed a persona of purity, a virgin Queen who was deeply loved by her people. The stress of leading a nation had not aged her at all. Abigail did not know if the combination of royal elegance and natural beauty came first or if the magnificent way the Queen ruled had contributed to her lovely demeanor. One thing she knew: if she had to decide how a queen should look, she would look exactly like Her Royal Highness.

This monarch had been surrounded by the beauty of the palace her entire life. Abigail considered this in her observations. She was struck by the contrasting components of Her Majesty's life. Again, the corridor had been filled with the cry of an empty anguished place deep within the Queen. And as always, this monarch rose, as though quickly forgetting the terrors of her sleep and steadied herself to embrace the matters of the day. Abigail blushed, suddenly growing aware that her pensive demeanor had been noticed. Sometimes, she felt as though her thoughts and feelings were easily read by the Queen. They smiled at each other and stood without a word, for the work of the day was at hand.

The Queen approached the palace meeting room and could not help noticing the atmosphere awaiting her. There was a different tone about the room this morning. Something was astir. She detected astonishment in the air as apparently her leaders shared a delicious new topic of discussion. Voices in the room were louder than usual and definitely eager to express their opinions on a newfound subject. These were the head men of her navy and the leaders who oversaw the trade and exportation of commodities that contributed to the extraordinary wealth of their country.

The spices and gold of Sheba were more abundant than any other country. Myrrh and frankincense were so sought after that their merchant ships and caravans never seemed to satisfy the demands of the trade routes. They were always gathering more ships and workers to keep up with the expanding business of this empire that extended to land on both sides of the Red Sea. The abundance of their natural treasure fueled the Queen with a solemn, earnest determination to steward these commodities with care and ensure that her people benefited from being citizens of such an affluent country.

Sheba had long enjoyed immense wealth. The Queen was eager for her subjects to reflect the riches of which they boasted. Should not such a nation have the happiest people, she pondered within. And yet often she spoke with downcast, disillusioned individuals whose eyes divulged the true story. Though the Queen often struggled over these dichotomies, she held her peace because of her awareness that of all people, she should have the satisfaction found in abundance. Yet her secret was that not even extravagant wealth satiated the longings she kept hidden well away. Musing to herself, she could not help thinking that she would rather experience the wars within surrounded by the wealth of Sheba than exist without such luxuries.

As usual, when announced, the Queen entered the room, and all was quiet. The formalities were completed quickly, and Ashor, head of her navy, began to speak. He started with all the routine procedures and gave his reports. Yet as he spoke, the Queen only wished he would reveal the topic they were discussing when she approached the room. She thought he would never end his monotonous speech.

Her patience grew thin. Interrupting, she spoke, "Ashor, is there nothing new to report? Please tell me the exciting news of the sea."

Ashor was a bit startled by her insistence. Although he had commanded the navy for the Queen many years, he still was often stunned by the intuitiveness of this monarch. He knew it to be genuine, yet never really understood it. "There are no special adventures to report, my lady."

He was aware of her love for stories of adventure brought back from places she had never been. The Queen looked at him intently, never saying a word, making him feel slightly uncomfortable. Although Sheba had long been ruled by women, he still felt uneasy when her eyes piercingly focused on him. He knew her to be a fair and compassionate ruler, and yet he was intimidated by her history of seeming to know who and what to probe. "My lady, there are no additional facts to disclose."

"Then what about rumors?" she asked with more intensity in her voice.

He was cornered once again. How did she always manage to ask the right question? And she knew better than anyone else that he would never lie to her.

"That's just it, my lady, there are no facts, only rumors. Why waste our time?" Ashor asked.

"I want to know these rumors that were giving all of you so much pleasure when I arrived," she spoke with an amused look on her face. There was silence. Realizing that he had no recourse, he began to tell her the rumors from the sea.

3

"What I am about to tell you, my lady, I heard myself only last night. When our myrrh ship returned from trade, after being at sea for months, the captain, Hagar, was anxious to report to us. When trading for silk, he met another merchant who asked him if he had heard about the land ruled by King Solomon.

"He reported that every country where he had been in port seemed to be astir, discussing the latest accounts of that kingdom. They speak of King Solomon. They speak of the people of Israel. They speak of a God. They speak of Israel's golden age, a nation united in purpose, described as peaceful and prosperous."

"Enough about vague generalities, tell me the details of what they say," interrupted the Queen.

"Please, dear Queen, remember this is secondhand, an unsubstantiated rumor at best."

"I will obviously take that into account," the Queen spoke in a tone that resembled a rebuke. "Please continue."

"According to Hagar, the merchant told him people from everywhere all over the earth were talking about this nation. Even kings are visiting because of the reports."

The Queen raised her eyebrows, feeling indignant. *This indeed is only a rumor*, she thought, *especially since I myself have never heard these reports.*

Ashor sensed the Queen's wandering thoughts. But since he did not know what else to do, he continued, "They say that there is no king like this king, that he exceeds all the kings of the earth in riches."

What? the Queen reacted, wondering how someone could say that. What gave him the authority to assess such a thing?

Ashor continued, "Solomon bows to the God of the Jews. The fame of Solomon and his God are spreading throughout the earth."

The Queen was perplexed. Why, this was unusual. She had never heard of a king who acquired fame because of his God. She herself gave credence to two chief deities, Ilmaqah and Ta'lab Riyam, as well as to other gods of her heritage, but this idea was totally new to her. She did not really understand. A strange curiosity began to stir. The wondering thoughts lured her toward some unknown inward place, but questions quickly approached to crowd them out. *This is scandalous*, she thought. How could I possibly be so intrigued by these mysterious rumors?

"Your Highness, are you all right?" questioned Ashor. "I mean, we are running way over our usual time."

Admittedly, she did feel overwhelmed. She acknowledged that perhaps they should continue their conversation later. She felt very vulnerable and tired. And to be honest, she had no idea why she was experiencing so many unusual emotions at the same time. Perhaps some food was in order to help her regain her bearings.

The men were puzzled by her persistent curiosity coming to such an abrupt halt. They highly regarded their Queen, but also had concluded it best not to try to figure her out. Without further ado, she left the room and was soon met by Abigail in the corridor.

"Just a light dinner," the Queen requested. "I need some time to myself."

"Would you like to take your meal in the courtyard?" asked Abigail, knowing that was one of the Queen's favorite places to eat.

"Why, that would be perfect," she replied.

The Queen loved Abigail's sweet smile. Her petite hand-maiden seldom made a suggestion that did not arise from a vivid awareness of all of her personal preferences. She served with much grace and had cultivated a unique charm that was evident in her quiet confidence.

Abigail centered her life around the Queen. She enjoyed her service to her. And even though Abigail knew the great affection she felt was mutual, seldom did they discuss the business of the kingdom. Like a large vault, the Queen's heart stored much. Tonight, Abigail noticed that she seemed unusually preoccupied as she entered the courtyard and shut the door behind her. *It must be such serious business, being a Queen*, Abigail concluded.

As soon as dinner was over, Abigail knew she had made a wise suggestion in encouraging the Queen to eat her meal in the open courtyard. The night was beautiful and the stars extraordinary. The Queen was visibly refreshed by the night breeze and private meal. Many dinners were spent entertaining dignitaries and ban-queting with visitors sent by heads of countries. In fact, tomorrow night would be another such event. It was good for Her Lady to have a quiet evening, Abigail observed. Perhaps she would even rest well tonight.

When the Queen reclined for the evening, she could not keep her thoughts from returning to the reports of Solomon's kingdom. The unusual stories of the evening only served to renew her desire to know more. *I should have asked additional questions,* she thought. Curiosity kept her mulling over and over what she had heard and trying to think of the best ways to find out further information. Lying on her bed, weariness overtook her. Just before her eyes closed, her thoughts turned to the banquet the next evening. Perhaps King Hiram would know about these happenings, and with that final thought, she drifted off to sleep.

4

Abigail awoke earlier than usual. The regularity of the Queen's dark dreams and awakening cries were alarming to her. Sometimes, she contemplated stories that had been passed down by the palace servants of the Queen's childhood. One legend told that as a child, the princess was to be sacrificed to a serpent god, but was rescued by a kind stranger. Could this kind of story indicate some sort of trauma that affected the Queen so deeply that she kept it locked away from everyone?

Many fables had been passed down about the Queen. She recalled the strange story of the Queen's mother, Queen Ismenie, who was supposedly possessed by a spirit, giving her the title of a jinni mother. Because of this, rumors had been conceived that her daughter had been born with the hooves of an animal. *How could people say such horrible things?* Abigail wondered. This story that the Queen had hooves was utterly unforgivable.

However, Abigail's own mother told her that Queen Ismenie was often awakened with night terrors, haunted by the fear of her gods, especially Ilmaqah, associated with the bull's head, whose image adorned the walls of the Marib temple. It was the blessing of Ilmaqah that was credited with Sheba's successful high dams and earthen wells that provided irrigation for their thriving agriculture and flourishing gardens. Queen Ismenie feared that if ever she displeased Ilmaqah, he would withdraw his blessings from Sheba. It was said that she lived in this anxiety until the day she died.

Just as in many other mornings, Abigail suddenly heard the loud cry of Her Lady. The scream sounded so urgent, so intense. An ache throbbed in Abigail's heart. She deeply cared about her Queen and wished that this night turmoil would come to an end. The cries had become her cue to quickly make her way into the Queen's chamber and do whatever she could to remove the dark heaviness from the room. This morning, she pulled the window ajar and gently pushed the curtain to the side to let in the morning sunlight. The fragrance of flowers outside the window entered the bedchamber, and soon, the aroma of fresh porridge served with special teas filled the air.

At first, the Queen allowed herself to wake up slowly. But once she recalled the events of the approaching evening, she was eager to begin her day. Having much to attend to for everything to be ready for the banquet, somehow, her duties felt easier with the anticipation of discussing Solomon with King Hiram of Tyre. If anyone would know if the reports were true, he would. He was a man who traveled much and always seemed to know what was going on in the world.

The day was busy, but for the Queen, her excitement about the evening grew. Abigail noticed a liveliness about the Queen and was comforted to see her with a brighter demeanor. The events of the day unfolded quickly. Meeting after meeting enabled the Queen to finally complete the last item on her list. The menu was complete, the entertainment approved, the decorations and the order of the evening decided. Behind this visit by King Hiram of Tyre was a business contract. The final negotiations had been settled upon and discussed with her best officers. She could think of nothing else to attend to except to ready herself for the evening.

Abigail had a new mix of spices for the rich ointment she applied generously to the Queen's skin, hoping the fragrance would prove to be refreshing. Again, she reflected on the Queen's loveliness. Her deep perceptive eyes and dark hair accentuated her face in such a way as to reveal her outward focus toward those she led. Her beauty was not drained by the demeanor of a self-indulgent woman. Sheba was fortunate to have her. She had won the hearts of most.

At last, there stood the pride and joy of Sheba, adorned in her royal attire. This evening, the pure white silk gown draped her tall, slender hourglass shape. The base of the skirt gathered to form a lush rounded trail behind her as she walked. Around her waist hung the most beautiful blue braided scarf, the fringes on the edges cascading down her gown. The longest tinsels almost touched the floor.

Wispy, sheer fabric fastened to the front of her gown draped over one bare shoulder, falling gracefully over her back. She wore a bold gold necklace and intricately carved bracelet, which encircled her upper arm, covered with the same jewels that were upon her crown. The Queen was a regal beauty, wearing her royal attire elegantly. She had definitely inherited the loveliness of her mother, Queen Ismenie.

"My lady, it is time, the guests are waiting," spoke Abigail. Off the Queen went so the festivities could begin.

The Queen made her entrance, her beauty taking away the breath of the onlookers. She began greeting the entourage of visitors who had graced her palace for the evening. Leaders of Sheba interacted with their visitors from Tyre. They spoke of many things and the night progressed smoothly. It was about time to be seated for dinner when the Queen could not help overhearing a small group discussing the temple that Solomon had built.

"Solomon!" The Queen's head turned. Did she hear that name spoken? Trying to maintain her composure, she tilted her head ever so slightly in their direction, hoping to hear the conversation. The visitor in the blue jacket was describing the opulent beauty and magnificence of the temple.

"I have never seen such grand architecture," she managed to hear as she continued to cautiously eavesdrop and overheard most of what they were saying. She was mesmerized. She could picture the carved figures of cherubs, palm trees, and flowers and the whole house within overlaid with pure gold, even the floor!

She found herself leaning ever more toward the men. She wanted to hear clearly the details of the skilled carpentry made with olive wood. Suddenly, she felt light-headed. It was only then that she realized the awkwardness of her stance. She wanted to ask them dozens of questions. *What am I doing?* she wondered, as she mechanically continued greeting the newly arriving visitors.

"Your Highness, all is ready for the guests to be seated, can I call everyone to dinner?" asked her head butler.

She nodded, then discreetly whispered in his ear, "Would you see to it that the gentleman in the blue jacket, who accompanies the king, is seated beside me?"

"Certainly, my lady," he spoke as he nodded. No questions were asked.

The instruments played and dinner was served. The Queen was seated between the King from Tyre and the gentleman in blue. His name was Caleb. She politely listened as the men spoke of their country, its future and dreams. They were happy to engage Sheba's queen in conversation. Grateful for the agreement she had made with them to export spices to their country, they found her to be a gracious hostess. She listened to them and at times advised them regarding Sheba's importing and exporting policies. She was excited to receive cedar and cypress timber from their country. Many citizens of Sheba would enjoy the products that could be made from these trees.

In the back of the Queen's mind, she really only wanted to discuss one thing: Solomon's kingdom. The reports she overheard Caleb speak of earlier gave her more reason to think there might be truth to the rumors from the sea. If these stories were true, she wondered why she was just now hearing them. She decided to approach her two guests with a sudden idea.

"King Hiram, would you and Caleb give me the honor of having tea with me after the banquet? We could meet in the courtyard and relax together, just the three of us. Perhaps we could discuss Solomon and his kingdom."

Instantly, they responded favorably, excitement breaking forth on their faces. The king seemed very lively in spite of the gray hair about his temples. She found it difficult to guess his age and noticed how comfortable he seemed in his flamboyant attire.

"We would be delighted, my Queen," answered King Hiram.

She nodded and arose to conclude the festivities. Although weary, she was rejuvenated by the thought of the tea and conversation to follow.

Finding her way into the courtyard, she noticed the stars were bright and the air crisp. She took a deep breath and enjoyed a moment of quiet. How she hoped to satisfy this unusual cavern of curiosity that had opened within her. Then through the door entered King Hiram and Caleb. They bowed and were seated.

"Relax, gentlemen," she spoke. "We have had a busy night."

The men surprised the Queen by their eagerness to continue their discourse on Solomon. First, the king spoke. "I will tell you what I know of Solomon, my lady. Caleb can tell you about the people of his kingdom, for he trades with them on a regular basis."

The king continued, "I first heard reports from my seamen. I sent my servants to validate what I heard, and to my surprise, King Solomon sent back for me. Out of respect for his father, I visited with the king. I always loved his father, David.

"Solomon's father had unusual qualities. He spoke of things I never quite understood. In his early years as king, David was obsessed about his God and told of his desire to behold Him. Others went so far as to call him a 'God-gazer.' I never really knew what that meant, but he loved it when his people were preoccupied with worshiping their God."

"Who is this God?" the Queen asked.

"Some call Him Jehovah," replied King Hiram. "It is said that their God did many great and powerful miracles for them throughout their history. He had ways of making His presence known to them, and they valued having this awareness of Him in their midst. There was an ark, a chest that they carried with them, which was known to be blessed with the very manifest presence of their God. This ark had become lost and was no longer among the people of Israel. Then, David retrieved the ark, and you cannot imagine the joy and celebration among the Israelites to once again have back this token of His presence."

He continued, "David erected a tabernacle to house the ark, and it was there that you could find the people worshiping, dancing, and speaking of the goodness of their God. You would have thought this would be enough for David. But until the day he died, he was preoccupied with building a temple where his God could make His tangible presence known to both the Israelites and all other people of the earth."

The Queen had no reason to doubt King Hiram. After all, he had known King David personally. However, the sound of it all was so foreign to her. The gods of her own country had names, but a presence? What exactly did that mean? Of course, she understood what it was like to be in someone's presence. You could see them, sense what they were like, and learn more of them with every exposure and interaction. But how could this apply to a god? She was mystified by the thought of a god who would come to his people in such a personal way.

She, as a queen, understood what it was like to be sought after by individuals who wanted an audience with her. They felt it a privilege to be in the presence of royalty. Then it came to her. That phrase "the presence of royalty" resonated deep within. Though she still knew nothing of the God of the Jews, she did understand a people who wanted to experience the presence of that which they treasured.

"My dear Queen, how easily I divert. Anyway, on the day that King David died, he gave of all his personal treasure to make sure a magnificent place would be built where all people could come and meet this God of the Jews. Solomon, although young and inexperienced at the time, inherited his father's ambition. He wanted a house where the knowledge of his God would be displayed. This was not a simple task, you know. The reason Solomon called for me was so that my country would provide cedar and cypress from Lebanon. He offered to pay my servants whatever wages I requested."

The Queen asked, "How could he make such a generous offer?"

"You will get your answer, Your Highness, by understanding the people of his kingdom. Never have I seen such a generous people. They willingly give of all that they have, for they feel they are giving out of what their God has freely given to them. I mean, they do not just give, but they are joyful, almost adoring in their loyal gestures.

"Yes, this was a business agreement, and yet Solomon could not even do business without discussing his God with exuberance and strength of spirit. Even I was filled with rejoicing and blessed his God who had given such a unique king to rule over his people.

"Let me be clear. Solomon is an astute administrator of business affairs. I will give you an example. He made a treaty with Pharaoh, king of Egypt. Solomon brought his daughter to Jerusalem, married her, and built her a house. Now he imports droves of horses and many chariots from her home country. It is said that Pharaoh's daughter loves to indulge in the luxuries of Jerusalem but resents being there because of a political alliance.

"When I made a treaty with Solomon, I gave him all the trees he needed and he gave me in return all the food that I could desire for my household. It was 480 years after the Israelites came from the land of Egypt, when Solomon began to build what he called The Lord's House. If you could see what he built! Seven years of bringing the best materials and the most skilled workers imaginable. Even more astonishing is beholding the king's face as he speaks about the truths buried in his heart, which spring forth like fountains proclaiming the perceived goodness of his God.

"All of his people say they are in awe of their king because they hear of the judgments he makes and see the wisdom in him to do justice. There is a passion in him that ignites his words like a fire of life and energy, which spreads throughout the lives of all his people. I can't explain it. I can only attest to it. Whatever has happened is extraordinary. Would you agree with me, Caleb?"

Caleb appeared immersed in the words of King Hiram, yet quickly nodded and continued where the king ended. "When I am there and see all the good that has been done in this place, I must confess, I tremble to my very core. Even as I speak of it now, there is a wonder that rises up in me. Perhaps their God is the true God." Caleb became quiet. There was a pure expression of openness and searching upon his face.

Caleb continued, "If ever I would choose another God to serve, I would choose one like this One. For you hear the reports of how good He is to His people, and then you see with your own eyes that these reports appear true in every direction. Extravagant, vast wealth, and flourishing, thriving life exist there like a well-watered garden. My lady, I feel weak as I speak of these things. Really, words cannot convey these truths. The real discovery is what happens inside when you are there beholding it all. It is a bit overwhelming. This has been a long day, Your Majesty. Do you mind if we rest for the night?"

The Queen had been awakened to a new hunger. But the dew of peace that rested upon her allowed her to graciously receive his suggestion. They almost reverently spoke their good-byes and began to depart.

"King Hiram," she quietly spoke. "I know that you have much business to finalize before your return. Could the two of you meet me again for a meal before your journey home? I will have food prepared, and perhaps we can continue our dialogue." She risked sounding too eager, she thought, but somehow that did not seem to matter.

5

When morning came, Abigail was tired. The banquet had created much extra work for her. She had planned to be up late, but the unscheduled meeting the Queen had with the guests kept her up even longer than she had anticipated. She wished she had felt as at ease as Her Lady appeared after her visit with the men of Tyre. However, her weariness did not stop her from her routine of rising early. Faithfully, she rose to prepare for the Queen's morning rituals. She saw to it that the tea and honey cakes were prepared, the clothes made ready, and the schedule for the day in place. For a moment, she sat in quiet and playfully twirled a strand of hair around her fingers.

Suddenly, she heard a crash coming from the Queen's bedchamber. She hurried down the hall and, as she entered the room, discovered the Queen in a state of disarray. Apparently in her sleep, she had flailed her arms and sent the water goblet beside her bed flying through the air, clattering against the wall and awakening herself in quite a stir.

When the Queen saw the look on Abigail's face, she realized that a remark from her might be helpful.

"Abigail, I am unharmed, just startled. I must have been having one of my restless nights and somehow managed to knock the golden goblet from the bedside table. I suppose that I might as well begin my day, since I am certain that I could never go back to sleep after all this commotion."

"Certainly, my lady," spoke Abigail as she cleaned the spilled water off the floor.

"Abigail, I do not know how you put up with me. Well, at least we will know that the floor has been recently cleaned," she spoke as she shook her head at the mess she had made.

"Thankfully, we don't start every morning this way, now do we, my lady," spoke Abigail. "There, there, I will be back right away with your tea and cake, and everything will seem brighter."

After several trips up and down the corridor, Abigail was filling the Queen's tea cup for the third time.

"Abigail, I would like to visit Uncle Hanam today. I have missed him lately and would love to have one of my heart-to-heart talks with him."

"I'm sure that he would be delighted to see you, my lady."

"I worry about him," continued the Queen. "I received a report yesterday that he seldom ever leaves his bed now. Apparently, his difficult spells are increasing. I make sure that he has the best of care, but I cannot erase the fact that he is very old and will never be the same as he was in his youth.

"I have such wonderful memories of him from my childhood. I always felt that I was his favorite, and I could talk to him about anything. How we laughed and played together! Yes, he has been a wonderful uncle to me. Once I lose him, I will have no more family. I must cherish what time I have left with him."

"I am so sorry to hear of his decline," spoke Abigail. "I have known that your relationship with him was special."

"Thank you, Abigail. Whenever I visit him, it does seem to cheer him. I am always grateful when he is able to engage again in one of our personal conversations. The staff informs me that he is becoming more incoherent with each passing day. They are hoping that a visit from me will help. And quite frankly, I feel that I need some time with him as well."

"Of course," replied Abigail.

The day continued according to routine and remained uneventful. Abigail arranged the Queen's schedule to her satisfaction and notified her when it was time to depart for her visit with Uncle Hanam. The Queen wrapped herself with her traditional head covering for the informal visit, not bothering with her crown.

The small grouping of camels transported the Queen discreetly to the ancestral home where she made sure that her beloved uncle had everything he needed. As they got closer to the family home, she could not help thinking of her father, King Agabo. After her mother died when she was ten years old, her father became the ruling Regent of Sheba. Then upon his deathbed, when she was only fifteen, he officially appointed her Queen of Sheba.

She would never forget that day. Her heart was broken into a thousand pieces. She felt so alone and overwhelmed by her new title. It was that very night that her nightmares began, on the day she first sat upon the alabaster throne resting upon the legs which resembled the hooves of a bull in honor of Ilmaqah. She felt a coldness rush through her body as she remembered his images upon the temple walls.

As a child, she always became fearful when she heard of her mother's nightmares. Once, she accidentally overheard her mother describing the shadows of bull heads that terrorized her. At that time, she prayed to the gods for protection, hoping she would not become prey to the oppressive terror experienced by her Mamma. On the day she became queen, the brokenness of her being and the onslaught of nightmares felt like more than she could endure.

Uncle Hanam was her sole comfort and support. He was all that was left of her family, and he tried valiantly to fill the huge void that accosted her. Now, over ten years later, she was having to let go of him bit by bit as she watched the demise of his mind and body.

They approached the complex of buildings, aged from their years, yet still beautiful. Arriving at the stately home, the Queen approached the grand entrance of the stone structure. Upon entering, she immediately recognized the familiar distinctive musty scent. She made her way toward the bedroom door and was met by his attendant.

"He has not been well, my lady. He has not been himself. Thank you for coming."

The Queen quietly entered the room. There upon the large four-poster bed lay her father's only living brother. He looked shriveled up and small in the center of the high ornate bed. His gray hair was matted and his beard scraggly. Once overweight, now he appeared far too thin and frail. Awakened by the noise of the squeaking door as it shut, he attempted to open his eyes.

As soon as he saw his dearest royal visitor, he tried to sit up in bed, immediately receiving help from the attendant.

"My lady, my beloved," he uttered in a frail voice.

The Queen walked to his side and kissed him upon his forehead.

"I have missed you, Uncle Hanam, I hope that you are rested for a visit."

"Always, with you," he responded, seeming to wake up a bit.

She signaled for the staff to leave and sat on the side of his bed.

"Shall we have one of our old-fashioned talks?" he asked, remembering some of their favorite moments together.

"I want to know about you. Tell me what is new in your life," Uncle Hanam spoke in his weakened voice. "I would be so pleased to learn what my favorite person has churning in her heart."

"Uncle Hanam, do you ever think about Mamma and Pappa?"

"Oh yes," he replied. "Until you, I had never met a woman as beautiful as your mother. To this day, it makes me sad that she lived in so much fear. And your father, how he loved to learn new things. Long after everyone was in bed, he would stay up, conversing with visitors and dignitaries through the night. He heartily enjoyed their stories."

With sadness in her eyes, she shared, "I miss them." She looked down for a moment then continued, "But on a more positive note, I still have you."

He looked kindly at her and replied, "I miss them too."

Unsure if she should approach the subject foremost in her mind, she decided to take a chance. She valued his opinion. He had been known in his youth to be a very intelligent man.

"Uncle Hanam, do you remember any stories of King David who had a son named Solomon?"

A few moments passed as he appeared to be focusing on the question.

"I remember little about Solomon, but I shall never forget a story I heard about King David. I remember because it was so unusual. Before he was king, he was a meager shepherd boy. It was he who killed a giant with his small slingshot when still just a young lad. The story goes that he also killed a lion and a bear with his bare hands." He rambled on, "Can you imagine, a shepherd boy becoming a king? I was quite entertained by these stories in my younger years."

"What do you know about the God of the Jews?" asked the Queen.

"The God of the Jews?" he repeated, raising his eyebrows, the left higher than the other as he attempted to open his one closed eye. His face contorted while he struggled to answer.

The sun must have disappeared behind a cloud, thought the Queen. The warmth of the sunlight dissipated as the room became dim and shadowy.

"The Jews and their God are no good," came his muddled reply. "Stay away from them. Promise me that you will never associate with the Jews." He grimaced and grabbed his head as though in pain, becoming incoherent and anxious upon the bed.

The Queen could tell that his mind was no longer with him. She was visibly shaken by his words. He had in the past been her favorite adviser. Now his response sounded more like the words of a mad man. Why should the mention of the Jews' God solicit such a hostile response?

Her uncle began to shake and yell unrecognizable words. Quickly, the attendants came back into the room.

"We are sorry that you have seen him this way, my lady."

The Queen nodded and swiftly left the room. She hurried to the palanquin, sat upon the cushions, and closed the curtains, quickly wiping away her tears. His words were deeply troubling. Perhaps she should have never brought up the subject. He had seemed like his old self initially. As she traveled back to the palace, she collected herself. She hoped she would never have to tell of the incident and dishonor her uncle.

Abigail prepared the Queen for bed. She could tell that the visit with Uncle Hanam had not gone well. Her Majesty had been withdrawn and quiet all evening. She thought that the anticipation of the meal planned for the next evening with the visitors from Tyre would lift her spirits, but apparently not. Something must have gone terribly wrong while the Queen was at the ancestral home.

Once Abigail had prepared the bed and was satisfied that she was no longer needed, she blew out the flames of all the lamps except for one candle beside the bed. She quietly left the room, leaving the Queen only with the sounds of the night coming from outside her window.

After making her usual rounds about the palace, eventually, Abigail retreated to her room where her husband Timothy already warmed himself beside the fire. Quickly, she joined him, happy that they could share some quiet moments together before they retired for the night.

How comfortable she felt beside her husband. They both shouldered much responsibility within the palace and understood the sacrifices made by the other because of their service. Timothy fulfilled his duties with excellence. Having been a personal guard for the Queen for many years, he now additionally was a trainer of others who joined the royal staff in such capacities.

Abigail studied his silhouette as they sat together beside the fire. She noticed the small scar on his jaw which had resulted from a miscalculated move during combat training many years earlier. Thank goodness, Timothy had never needed to utilize these skills to protect the Queen. They both served in their assigned areas with loyal hearts. This same superb quality served them well in their marriage. The tender devotion in which they fulfilled their roles outside of their relationship was a reflection of how they served each other.

"Abigail, my love, you seem so pensive tonight. Tell me about your day," Timothy said.

She let out a sigh of relief at the invitation to share what was on her heart. "I know that we have discussed this before, but I cannot find relief from my concerns for the Queen. Sometimes, I wonder if her night terrors will ever end. And it seems that even if she is not awakened by one of her nightmares, her restless nights are still apparent. Just this morning, she flailed in bed so violently that the water goblet was thrust clear across the room and awoke her as it smashed against the wall. For years, these recurring episodes have become common. I thought they could not get worse, but this past year has proved me wrong. And recent weeks have brought me to tears more times than I care to recount. I am so concerned for her."

Timothy reached for her and drew her to himself. He understood better than anyone the love she had for Her Majesty. No one knew the personal life of the Queen like Abigail did.

Known by all to be gallant and courageous, Timothy was quick on his feet and strong as anyone could ever hope to be. And yet the attribute that had comforted and strengthened Abigail the most over the years was his protectiveness of her. She was certain that he would lay down his life on her behalf if ever needed.

Timothy gently rubbed her arm as she laid her head upon his shoulder. "It is difficult to understand such things," he spoke. "We must pray to the gods that they will bring her the help she needs."

After a moment of quiet, he continued, "Always remember, my love, that you need not know the answers for her. Your love for her is your gift. You are a strength and constant reminder to her that she is not alone."

Abigail finally felt herself relax. Timothy was her rock. He always knew what to say to calm her fears.

"Let's go to sleep," she spoke as she took his hand. "Tomorrow may be a new beginning."

Together, they prepared for bed, as they had so many times before. Slipping beneath the covers, Timothy wrapped his arms around her, and she drifted off to sleep beside him in her favorite secure place.

6

It occurred to Abigail that the Queen was sleeping later than usual. In some ways, this made sense. She must have been exhausted from her visit with Uncle Hanam. Abigail felt relieved that she could enjoy a little extra time before the business of another day. She sat down to her own cup of tea and took some nourishment, sampling some leftover dainties from the banquet the night before.

When she reached to catch some crumbs that she swept from the table into her hand, she heard the ringing of a bell. She hesitated. Again, the bell rang. The jingle of the bell resounded down the hallway. It had been months since she heard the Queen ring for her. The melodious sounds of the golden hand-held instrument were so different from the shrill cries that had become the norm of the Queen's morning risings. Abigail collected her thoughts. *My lady must have had pleasant dreams*, she thought to herself as she hurried down the corridor. When she entered the chamber, she was surprised that the Queen appeared to have been awake for a while. Abigail was quite confused, actually, and curious to know what was happening.

"Good morning, Abigail, it is so good to see you," the Queen spoke.

Abigail, though smiling, was a bit taken aback by all of this. The heaviness of the nightmares was noticeably absent from the room. She opened the door for the food to be brought in and was quite honestly having difficulty processing all of this.

The Queen appeared elated and began to speak, "Something astonishing has happened. Please be seated. You know better than anyone about the horrible night terrors that continually assault me."

Abigail was stunned. The Queen had never spoken about any of this with her, although her haunting cries had made their reality awkwardly known.

Seeing the surprise on her face, the Queen said, "I know that we have never spoken of these things, and yet today, I must. The outburst caused by my oppressive sleep has always been the culmination of such dark nightmares that I have never wanted to discuss them with anyone. These dreams have been vividly real and frightening, filled with ghostly figures and hostile words. My villains literally seemed to assault and harness me by their strength, leaving me unable to defend myself as I sank to the black bottoms of the ocean, never to breathe again. I wrestled to break free but could not."

Tears filled her eyes as she continued to speak with determination in her voice. "I tried to escape, believe me, I tried. Only waking could momentarily rescue me from the dark suffocation and sense of imminent death. But last night, last night," she stuttered as she grasped the right words. "I was having this same nightmare. The darkness and feeling of helplessness was stronger than ever. I was bound and ever falling into that excruciating deep pit of darkness." The Queen began sobbing.

Abigail could not anticipate what would come next. She had not once ever seen the Queen cry like this. What on earth was happening?

"Abigail," she spoke, struggling for the words. Stumbling over her own emotions, she managed to continue, "Something happened, some kind of divine intervention, an unseen deliverer arrived. I could not see the identity of the force, but somehow, I perceived righteous anger toward the darkness that tried to steal my life from me. This power had the amazing strength to avenge me. It was as though an invisible hand grabbed me and cut off every trace of evil that was trying to destroy me. In an unnatural, I suppose supernatural way, I was carried to a place where I could breathe again."

The Queen gasped deeply as though for the first time. "Abigail, I felt free. For a glorious few moments, I felt a freedom, a release, a peace that even now I am unable to describe." Tears ran down her cheeks. She stood and embraced her beloved attendant.

Such emotion rose up within Abigail that she feared she would burst wide open. She managed to whisper, "I am so happy for you, so very happy."

The Queen wiped her tear-stained cheeks and saw the steady flow of tears upon Abigail's face. They shared yet another moment of quiet bonding that would never be forgotten as long as they lived.

"Abigail," said the Queen, "I have held in my heart a desire to give you something that is very special to me. As you know, I have no family except Uncle Hanam. But you have always been with me. My dearest friend, I want you to have this." She opened a drawer and Abigail saw a beautiful gold necklace from which hung a tiny ornate golden ornament in the shape of a house topped with stones.

Abigail's mouth dropped. The necklace was one of the most beautiful she had ever seen. Often, this small dangling charm was referred to as a "house of the soul" to the citizens of Sheba.

"My lady, surely this family keepsake must not depart from you," spoke Abigail.

The Queen smiled. "I have thought of this for some time. I remember it upon my mother's neck as a child when I sat on her lap and laid my head against her. I must give it to you as a reminder of all the times we have shared our hearts and souls with each other." She took the ornamental chain from the drawer and fastened it around Abigail's neck.

Abigail did not know what to say. She looked into the face of the Queen, and the sweetest smiles spread upon both of their faces. "I will wear this always with endearing thoughts of you, whether we are together or apart."

The Queen replied, "May it always be a token of our enduring friendship."

When they turned to go their separate ways, the Queen paused.

"Abigail, sometimes I wonder if I will ever meet a man that I could be as comfortable with as I am you. I desire an heir and the companionship of a husband. Yet I am so consumed with my role as Queen that I fear I have become detached from personal ambitions."

"My lady," Abigail spoke, "the day may come when your heart is reawakened to these longings you have hidden away."

The peace of the mystical dream that abruptly broke the cycle of terror remained with the Queen. She certainly did not understand what had happened. What was behind such power, such kindness, such redemptive aid? She considered the amazing moment of peace she enjoyed. She wanted to know who or what was behind the unusual encounter. *To live the rest of her life with the companionship of tranquility and hope would be beyond imagination*, she thought to herself. Whoever could be privileged to live in such a way?

7

The rays of the sun sparkled through the branches of the courtyard trees with their warmth resting upon the Queen's face. She waited quietly for her guests. Where would their conversation transport them today? This strange new adventure had definitely taken on a life of its own. Only days ago, she had never heard of the reports of Solomon and his God called Jehovah. Now, not only had she heard, she knew she must know more!

The palace fountains and surrounding flowers were indeed breathtaking. Every detail of the courtyard had been considered and carefully crafted for the comfort of palace guests. The sacredness of hospitality was a serious matter for Shebeans. So sacred was the custom that if a guest shared a meal with you, the qualities of a covenant relationship were assumed. If you supped with a friend, the anticipation was that of friendship, enjoyment, rest, refreshment, peace, safety, provision, kindness, and satisfaction. This was true whether in a meager abode or a palace. You could assume to be safe in the home of such an intimate friend. All that belonged to the host was at the disposal of their guests. From the washing of the feet of the visitors upon arrival, to the aromatic oils upon their head, to the satisfying of their hunger, the rituals of hospitality sought to satisfy every need.

The courtyard fountain was carefully placed at just the right angle to catch the delicate breezes and cool palace guests as they enjoyed the beauty of the flowering garden tapestries. Much attention was given to create beauty in the courtyard so that visitors would be inwardly, as well as outwardly, refreshed. The ultimate insult would thus be to betray someone you had shared hospitality with in your home. For it was in this context that intimate relationships were formed.

The Queen reflected on the meaning of eating together. She found it most interesting that this would now be her third time of sharing hospitality with these visitors from a faraway land. It was rare for the Queen to devote so much of her time with guests for the business of her kingdom was very demanding. These unusual circumstances certainly reflected a switch of focus in her heart as she ventured into new territories.

The doorkeeper ushered the guests in as the Queen greeted them. The brightness of their faces added to the pleasure of once again meeting to discuss what they had seen and experienced of the kingdom of the Jews. The atmosphere of this paradise nestled within the innermost part of the palace was the perfect place for such conversation. They richly enjoyed the food and drink, eagerly anticipating their interaction afterward. Even the present seemingly trivial talk of trade and commerce seemed tolerable in such pleasant surroundings.

The conversation of the previous night had mainly been dominated by King Hiram. Since little had been heard from Caleb, Her Majesty's thoughts turned to him.

"Caleb," spoke the Queen, "would you do me the honor of sharing what you have learned of the children of Israel?"

Caleb had the habit of always nodding when he was addressed. He had observed that this royalty of Sheba was an eloquent speaker and had enjoyed the sound of her melodious voice. His quiet nature made him a little more hesitant than King Hiram to contribute, but he felt it his duty to respond to her inquisitive disposition.

Slightly blushing, he began, "My lady, I have never met King Solomon. I have only seen him from afar and heard of him through his people. But as strange as this might sound to you, it is his people, who have forever affected my view of his kingdom. Have you ever met an ordinary person who had an extraordinary effect on you? Mind you, I am speaking of sailors, merchants, hardworking people. In fact, it is through this humble array of faces that I have glimpsed a way of life before unknown to me. It is through such vessels that the reports have traveled reaching kings and kingdoms all over the world."

Dressed in subdued colors and obviously very shy, Caleb was nonetheless off to a good start. Even his effort to maintain eye contact with the Queen seemed to become easier for him. "For example, I shall never forget the cook who lived on a ship of Solomon's fleet. His face was blackened from years of hard toil in the kitchen preparing the food for all on board the ship, but the sweetness of his inner person shone forth like a lighthouse. He felt no disdain for his position. To the contrary, he was honored to be an Israelite. He was a good man, though uneducated, so it was difficult for him to communicate. Yet with great poise and strength, he conveyed his message.

"If you mentioned Jehovah, he lit up and could not stop telling you what he knew of Him. I was shocked that he spoke of God like you would a personal friend. He himself was at the dedication of the temple, and when he discussed it, both tears and smiles branded his face.

"The cook tried to explain to me what he experienced there. He relayed that Solomon prayed for the people upon a bronze scaffold, set in the midst of the temple court. There, Solomon stood, then knelt upon his knees before all of Israel, and spread forth his hands toward heaven, saying, 'Oh, Lord, there is no God like You in the heavens or in the earth, keeping covenant and showing mercy and loving kindness to Your servants who walk before You with all their hearts.'"

Hanging on to his every word, the Queen's mind was churning. She considered the gods of Sheba. Compared to the God of the Jews, hers seemed like cold, empty statues which might respond if the stars were aligned just right or the superstitious requirements were satisfied perfectly. But these Israelites spoke using words like "love" and "kindness" to describe their God. These were the warm traits of someone who deeply cared.

Her mind was not accustomed to such ideas pertaining to a god. The affections of the Jewish people were focused on one God as though no other gods existed. This was definitely not the way of her people. Momentarily, she felt guilty for betraying her normal orientation to spiritual things, but her thoughts were quickly interrupted as Caleb continued.

"Solomon prayed and prayed for the people that day. He addressed absolutely everything pertaining to their lives and exuded exceptional confidence that God heard his prayers and would answer. He believed that the Israelites would walk in the ways of Jehovah as long as they lived. The prayer was quite enthralling," said Caleb.

"The king left no stone unturned, and I suppose the Israelites had never felt so bombarded with prayer. The baker thought the king would never end, but he said the longer King Solomon prayed, the richer the atmosphere became with joy and tenderness.

"Just about the time Solomon was done with his supplications, he began to pray for those who would visit. Apparently, he sensed that many strangers would hear about Jehovah and come from near and far to experience his God. He asked Jehovah to answer the prayers of the strangers who came, so that all people of the earth might know Him.

"As the cook spoke with me, I knew that he shared Solomon's heart. For I could see in his demeanor that he sincerely wanted me to know his God. He told me that his own life would never be the same since knowing Jehovah. I was shaken. The testimony came from a common man of little worldly status. Yet it was men of his likeness who joined the ranks of influential giants and were turning the world upside down by their attestation of the great-ness of their God," Caleb said.

"They take this message with them into ports, to faraway places, and as a result, from the simplest of people to the most regal of rulers—they are all traveling to find out if the reports they hear are true. This lowly cook had the traits of distinguished nobility. He was proud of his inner treasure and gave it away wherever he went. My heart was affected by his words like none I had ever heard before. My lady, this is just one of the faces I will never forget in a sea of many. There is something different about those who have encountered this God they call Jehovah."

The Queen's mind became fixed on one part of what she heard. She replayed the words in her mind over and over: "They are all coming to find out if the reports they hear are true...to find out if the reports they hear are true...if they are true...if they are true." She did not know how long she had been obsessing over these words, but she could feel the quizzical looks peering at her from the faces of her guests.

All of a sudden, she burst out in laughter. Stunned, her guests looked at her in a questioning manner. Then she began to laugh even more heartily. The men became rigid as though not quite sure what to do. They beheld her carefree demeanor and then, without warning, began to laugh as well. The minutes passed, and like children, they engaged in the sport of laughing until they were wonderfully weary from its hold upon them.

The guests knew they should go, already having delayed their departure to satisfy the Queen's request for another visit. None of them had even considered beforehand that their interactions would end in this seemingly frivolous manner. Why were they laughing? Honestly, they had no idea. For whatever the reason, an unusual atmosphere engulfed them. Until their last good-bye, all three enjoyed the warmth and gaiety that flooded them. The Queen sat in wonder at these indescribable happenings while she watched them depart. Would she ever see King Hiram and

Caleb again? One thing was certain: she would never forget the unspeakable joy that visited them that day.

Abigail, aware that the visitors were leaving, promptly resumed her post where she would reunite with the Queen and discuss the remaining daily agenda. She watched Her Lady approach and observed that a heaviness seemed to have vanished from her. Where were the lines typically pronounced between her eyebrows after a long meeting? Where was the intensely pre-occupied expression that usually followed serious conversations? Abigail felt certain that she had heard the entire group laughing robustly together. These were certainly unusual times, new to this palace home.

The Queen addressed her cheerfully, "Take some time for yourself or spend some time with Timothy. Relax and forget your responsibilities for the afternoon. As for me, I wish to take a walk. I will be behind the palace in the walled areas of the gardens."

Noticing the alarm on Abigail's face, she spoke reassuringly, "I'll be fine, but if it makes you feel better, you may place a guard near the gate entrance."

In the solitude of the palace acres, the Queen of Sheba walked for hours. What had happened to her over the years? She was so focused on her responsibilities that she could not even remember a time that she was this relaxed and actively enjoying her life. In fact, she surmised, perhaps she had no life apart from ruling Sheba.

Breathing the fresh air and walking among the majestic trees planted by long-past ancestors, she felt pleasure as she absorbed the surrounding beauty. She drank in the tranquility and melodious sounds of the glistening gardens. Strange, how all of this was right under her nose, yet day after day, year after year, she lived unaware.

For a moment, she felt a slight sense of sadness attempt to surface as she began to realize how much she had been missing by ignoring these gifts around her. But now, she caught a glimpse of what she had lacked. As though her surroundings discerned her thoughts, everything around her seemed to compensate by revealing their vibrant brilliance to her. Never had the air seemed crisper, the trees greener, the noises clearer.

This surrounding sanctuary called to her, beckoning her to visit more often. Certainly, coming to this place more regularly would clear her mind to help make good decisions for Sheba. Perhaps, even she could be seen by other nations to be a wise leader, like Solomon. For now, that seemed like an out-of-reach objective. She meandered back to the palace where her duties awaited.

The Queen began to grow accustomed to her newfound peace, almost protective of it, lest she be abandoned by its companionship. Others noticed the change. The calmness upon her seldom was disrupted. Yes, she still had many questions. She continued to face many challenges, but some things she desperately hoped would never be the same. Weeks had passed by since the mysterious encounters. However, she knew one thing, what had happened within her was not over. There was more...

8

Having arranged an early appointment with Ashor, the Queen made her way to the meeting. Her time with him lately had been full of business concerning the navy. There was always something new to discuss, another problem to solve, or new opportunities to sort. She knew that Ashor made many decisions without her. She trusted him and his discretion. He had learned what would be important to bring before her and what to tackle on his own. She wished that she could promote him to a better position, although his current rank was already among the highest.

The palace cabinet chamber seemed an odd place to discuss with Ashor what was on her mind this day. The two of them sat at the huge oval table. Comfortable in each other's presence, the Queen wasted no time.

"Ashor, I will be frank. I want to travel to Jerusalem."

Often when in thought, Ashor laid his forefinger on his cheek and rested his chin on his folded hand. At length, he put down his hand and responded with a concerned expression on his face, "My lady, I don't know what to say. This is very unusual. It is a daring venture. You could encounter much peril, danger, and definitely uncomfortable inconveniences not common for a queen."

He thought back throughout the history of Sheba and could not remember a ruler ever embarking on such a journey. Yes, they often sent royal representatives on their behalf, but this, this was an entirely novel idea. Was it even in the best interest of the country? Shebeans needed her at home. What if a national crisis arose? Not to mention, what would the people think of her? On first reflection, this seemed such an irresponsible idea. Why couldn't she choose someone to go on her behalf like other monarchs? Was she herself? What was she thinking?

The Queen continued, "Many kings have visited there, why not I?" She looked at him very seriously, waiting for his answer.

"Your Highness, perhaps others such as yourself have had the good fortune of being more conveniently located to Jerusalem. You live very far away, about a six-month journey. You would have to travel in harsh desert conditions unrelenting in their extreme temperatures. And you know we only have camels that can endure the toughness of the trip. A very large caravan of travelers would be needed to transport a queen, and their lives would be subjected to danger as well. The reports of desert travel are concerning.

"Thieves and bandits hide out to prey upon vulnerable sojourners. My specialty, of course, is the navy. But the reports of the desert journeys have always raised apprehension within me. It would take months to get there and months to return. If you embarked on this journey, you would sacrifice much."

The Queen had known that Ashor would speak his mind frankly. However, she was not quite prepared for the weight of his discouraging words. "Ashor," she replied, "I will consider what you have spoken." She arose, nodded, and left the room.

It was not unusual for them to have brief discussions, but Ashor somehow knew this one was not over. In recent weeks, he had observed the changes apparent upon the Queen's countenance. Having served with her many years, he knew that something had profoundly affected her. Yet he was caught off-guard by the announcement of this dramatic idea of undertaking such a dangerous journey. For some time after the Queen departed, he remained seated, contemplating what had been said.

When the Queen left the meeting, she was met by Abigail, who began to relay a message that had been delivered to the palace while she met with Ashor. "A courier arrived and said that your Uncle Hanam is urgently requesting that you go to him. He has something important to say to you."

The look on the Queen's face spoke volumes to Abigail. The restrained and yet concerned expression was obvious.

"Abigail, have a small private meal brought to my bedchamber while I consider his request."

The Queen was still recovering from the words of Ashor. Now must she be subjected to Uncle Hanam, especially if he was not himself? She still was not accustomed to protecting her heart from him. Such joy had come to her from his words over the years. She wished for the times of old, when she was completely safe with him. Nevertheless, she must go. What if he was dying and had parting words for her?

She traversed the familiar road once again to her ancestral home, the location of many memories. Arriving at the entrance, she wished that she could just focus on her increasing desire to travel to Jerusalem. Instead, she had to brace for the unknown as she approached Uncle Hanam's room.

"How is he today?" she asked the guard outside the door.

"I am not certain," came the reply. "He has seemed alert but quiet. You must be the judge, my lady."

As she entered his room, his good eye was opened wide, and apparently, he had been anxiously awaiting her.

"I received your message," she began, leaning to kiss his forehead.

"I hope that all is well with you," she spoke as they were left alone in the room.

"Oh yes, oh yes!" He surprised her by his enthusiastic response. "I have some good news!"

Already feeling a bit perplexed, she did not know what to expect next. "And what would that be?" she asked, not sure if she really wanted to hear what he had to say.

Bluntly, he began to speak, "Last night in a dream, the gods spoke with me and told me that you are to go to Jerusalem." His face brightened like a magician with a hidden surprise.

Totally unprepared for what she heard, she gripped her face in her hands. Did she hear him correctly? Did he not just ask her on her last visit to promise that she would never affiliate with the Jews? Why did she feel confused at this seemingly good news? She wanted to embrace his words, but restrained herself. She had to guard her heart.

She observed the look of delight on his face. Without a moment's hesitation, he continued, "Yes, yes, you must go to Jerusalem, and I will rule in your absence," his voice becoming louder with each word. "Next of kin, blood of your blood, the gods have told me that I must rule!" he concluded while tilting his head slightly to the side with a sly adversarial stare upon his face.

Just when she thought her situation could not feel more oppressive, it did. What on earth was happening? How could he address the very desire of her heart, speaking what she would have yearned to hear from him, yet in a manner that flooded her with fear and confusion? Was he trying to intimidate her? Was he trying to prevent her from going? Was he her enemy? Was he her loving uncle? Who was he? No, this could not be happening to her.

Her face, still held between her hands, felt damp from perspiration. Deliberately trying to calm her emotions, she reminded herself that the voice she heard was not her uncle. The expression she saw was not her uncle. Trickery, deception, partial truth cloaked in lies, strange enemies of an unknown origin were all that he spoke.

Emotionless, she rose and called for the attendant. "He is not well today." As she abruptly left the room, she saw that her uncle was fast asleep, as though he never even knew the conversation happened.

Darkness was descending upon the palace when the Queen arrived. She entered and, when met by Abigail, had little energy, even for small conversation. "Abigail, I am not hungry. I think I will go to bed early tonight. Give me a little time alone and then we will prepare to retire for the evening."

"Yes, Your Majesty."

Slowly, the Queen walked to her room. The doors closed and Abigail heard her sobbing. *Life has felt unusually dramatic within the palace walls recently*, thought Abigail. She found herself hoping that the night terrors would not return again, especially since she did not understand what was causing the Queen such distress.

9

The next day, passing through the palace hallways, the Queen headed for Abigail, who was busy directing the palace attendants. The Queen spoke, "Have the camels made ready at once. I intend to go to Mahram Bilqis." Seeing the look of surprise on Abigail's face, she spoke again, "Mahram Bilqis, the Temple Awwam."

"Yes, Your Majesty," she answered as she made haste. Of course, Abigail knew the Temple, but usually, the palace staff was given more advanced notice. The tasks involved to make ready for a venture away from the palace grounds were not small. The Queen rested in her quarters until given notice they were ready for her departure.

Nestled outside the city, the temple was the place of worship for the Sabaean religion. The Queen, who was always there for special occasions, had never been known to go alone. Even so, Abigail did not question the decision, for everyone who knew Her Highness concluded her to have a brilliant mind and to make discerning decisions.

Approaching the camels, the Queen observed how tall and stately were the hardy animals. They were draped in beautiful colored fabric which rested beneath the oak saddles. Accompanied by her trusted armed guard, Timothy, she entered the royal palanquin. They made their way around the city toward the temple which rose on the horizon as a magnificent architectural silhouette.

Sheba is splendid, she thought, as they passed by another beautiful garden. The agriculture flourished, thanks to the very high dams and large wells which provided them irrigation and hydraulic power. Some of the dams were several stories high.

Having arrived, the Queen had a solemn expression on her face as she approached the entrance to the temple. Here she had participated in many religious ceremonies, paying homage to the numerous gods of her heritage. Her people were steadfast in their traditions and did not waiver in their tribute to Sheba's deities. She entered the temple, and she sat in solitude. The quiet surrounding her was almost eerie, a feeling new to her in this setting.

Her thoughts became focused on Sheba's chief deity, Ilmaqah, the masculine sun-god. Her eyes focused as she scanned the temple walls. She observed the motifs associated with Ilmaqah: the bull's head, the vine, and also the lion's skin on a human statue.

Ilmaqah was their god of agriculture and irrigation, which was the basis of successful farming in this oasis capital. The god's animal attributes were the bull, and in later times, the vine symbol emerged. A protector of artificial irrigation, Ilmaqah was lord of the temple of the Sabaean federation of tribes. The religion of Sabianism was the worship of the host of heaven: sun, moon, and stars; and it originated with Sheba.

Why was she revisiting this sacred history in her mind? Hoping that stillness would guide her as a friend, the Queen quieted her thoughts and sat in silence in the familiar surroundings. The depth of her soul reached for an answer to the cry of her heart.

Then out of her being came forth whispered words of prayer. "To whom I am addressing, I know not, but I want you to know I have need of thee. I need thy perfect wisdom. The wealth of Sheba abounds, yet it is thy blessing I seek, thy riches, thy understanding.

"You, the one who defended me and lifted me out of my pit of terror, I call to you. In my asking, shall I be given? In my seeking, shall I find? In your cloak, shall I be safe? Who are you to whom I call? I reach for your response. I seek to find you. Come from your hiding place and open the eyes of my understanding. Come, come, come…show me, show me." As the words slipped from her lips, she felt a treasure trove of peace.

Her flow of words ceased, and the Queen felt a tender satisfaction culminating inside her heart. She opened her eyes, anticipating the whole temple to be flooded with the warmth she felt within. But to her surprise, it was to the contrary. Held within the confines of the ornate walls was an odd stony coldness that threatened to unsettle this sacred moment. She felt a sudden shiver, and her eyes began to scan the temple. She froze in fear as she saw the narrowed eyes of the bull staring at her. Involuntarily, a rush of repulsion rose up in her. A coldness encircled her, bearing the familiar resemblance of the ghostly darkness of the night terrors. Stunned, her survival instincts rose, and she sought to escape this feeling of impending threat. With a rush of energy, she wanted to run.

"Wait, wait," she said out loud. "I must steady myself, I'm here to find solace, not reminisce eerie dreams of my past." She closed her eyes again and sought the stability she felt so resolutely only moments before. Abruptly, she was struck by the realization of how aloof the tokens of the gods seemed as they surrounded her. How cold and impersonal they appeared while she sat alone as their sole audience.

She pondered her instincts for what seemed like a long time. Then she began to rehearse the testimonies of those who attested to the reality of the Jews' one true God. They spoke of Him as a personal God who embraced his subjects with love. What a contrast to her feelings when peering upon the gods of her heritage. Then she knew the answer to the questions she sought. It was crystal clear. Yes, yes, yes, it would be good to meet Solomon, hear his wisdom, and see his kingdom. Perhaps, his wisdom would be the guiding light she sought that would benefit all of Sheba.

But even more prominent in her thoughts were the unanswered questions about Solomon's God. If He was the true God, then, no, she could not bear to think of it, but if it was true, then all that she knew of her gods was false. If Jehovah was the only true God, then all of Sheba was deceived. The unimaginable regret that came with this thought crushed her. And it was in that moment she knew for certain that she must go to Jerusalem and find out for herself. She had her answer.

The Queen jumped to her feet as one who had been summoned on a pilgrimage, a divine commission. Now out of her conflict, she exited the temple a resolute woman. Her decision was irrevocable. She would travel to Jerusalem.

Later at the palace, the Queen, already reclining for the evening, could not stop her thoughts from racing. The day, she knew, had been an important crossroad and now she was entering into unknown territory. Who could best help her chart this course? She recalled her meeting with Ashor. His words returned to her, "My specialty has been the seas, but the reports of the desert journeys have always raised apprehension within me."

Ashor was as loyal as any countryman could be. But certainly the desert routes would be unfamiliar to him. Of course, he would feel protective of her lofty ambitions.

Instantly, she knew she should meet with Tamrin. Although she did not have the same personal history with him as Ashor, he definitely was her expert for expeditions by land. The leader and architect of all her trade caravans, Tamrin owned many hundreds of camels, mules, and asses, with which he journeyed as far as India. Inspired by the possibility of a satisfactory solution, she drifted off to sleep.

10

Abigail was in a flurry of activity. The morning seemed to speed by too quickly. She had awakened on a set course, only to have it unraveled by the Queen. Every appointment had to be canceled. New appointments were set up. Out of the storm of rearranging came the meeting required by Her Majesty.

The sun shone brightly upon the palace windows. The sparkling rays of light warmed the meeting room for Ashor and Tamrin as they settled in their chairs. Amazingly, they both had been able to attend this meeting that seemed so urgent to the Queen. Abigail was pensive as she considered the forcefulness of the Queen's intentions. It was spoken of Her Lady that she ruled with the heart of a woman as well as the forcefulness and courage of a man.

Abigail opened the door for the entrance of Sheba's noble queen, their eyes meeting as they exchanged a reassuring glance. Again, Abigail was reminded of how blessed she was to work closely with this slender yet commanding Queen, who was obviously on some newly found adventure.

The three distinguished leaders greeted one another. Immediately, the Queen noticed Ashor's reserved manner. It appeared that he must have pondered the effects of his words on her when they last met. She knew him to be as sensitive as he was strong. Caught up in the excitement of her new venture, the discouragement of their last encounter felt far away.

"I have gathered you here for an important matter," she began. "I know that it might come as a surprise to you, but I have been quite impacted by the reports of Solomon that have come from Jerusalem."

Ashor looked down as she continued, "I have carefully considered and have come to the conclusion that I must go there." She deliberately looked in the direction of Tamrin, anxious to interpret his response.

Calmly, Tamrin responded, "Well, of course, I understand why you would be compelled to journey there." Tamrin, a rather large man, a risk-taker, had enjoyed his many travels.

She quickly looked at Ashor and saw the look of surprise on his face. She hoped that her own feelings were well hidden. Tamrin continued, "You know that I have traded with Israel, taking gold, ebony, and sapphires to Solomon for use by his hundreds of carpenters and masons who were building the great temple of Jerusalem."

The Queen, quite stunned, began to put the pieces together. The rumors, the excitement of the men of her navy; well, it had never occurred to her that some of what they had heard came from the travels of one of her own leaders.

For a moment, dumbfounded, she simply reconsidered his words, "Well, of course, I understand why you would be compelled to travel there." It took her a moment to find composure from the weight of the good news she heard. She looked out the palace window at the spectrum of colors dazzling in the sun's rays throughout the garden. She listened to the peaceful sounds of the spectacular fountain. A blissfulness filled her heart. Ashor and Tamrin were struck by the Queen's calm countenance as a subtle smile emerged across her face. She began to speak, "So, Tamrin, you have been there, you must tell me more!"

11

Each morning, Tamrin met with the Queen and relayed all that he knew about Solomon. In the afternoons, they would finalize additional plans for the journey. Tamrin and Ashor became increasingly confident that the Queen's desire to encounter Solomon was strong enough for her to embark on the immense journey across the desert sands, along the coast of the Red Sea, up to Moab, and into Jerusalem. Such a journey would require at least six months' time each way, since camels could only travel a short distance each day.

They would need a minimum of four weeks to prepare for the journey, Tamrin advised. They must decide upon gifts to carry to King Solomon and make all the preparations needed for a caravan fit for a queen. This was the first such occasion for Sheba. Also, the Queen must make plans for governing while she was away. And last, but not least, she must speak to her people. They hoped that four weeks would allow time for the attention needed to accomplish these and additional details. Conversing and planning with Tamrin fueled her passion to press forward in spite of the unknown challenges that might be ahead.

The Queen tossed in bed. Her sleeplessness was the perfect breeding ground for restless thoughts. She wondered at how lonely she felt at this time, even though the doors had opened widely for the trip she had ached to take. She knew that the wind of her sails had temporarily waned, yet her resoluteness had not. The next important decision to be made weighed heavily upon her. Someone had to be in charge of Sheba while she was away. That "someone" had to be one of her leaders she wholeheartedly trusted. Several options churned in her mind throughout the night. She drifted off to sleep occasionally, but the restless thoughts continued until morning.

Exhausted, she arose early. Abigail brought her porridge and gave her ample time to prepare for the day. Given a message for the Queen, she promptly began, "My lady, Ashor has requested to speak with you as soon as possible. Should I delay your morning meeting with Tamrin?" Relieved that Abigail had offered the suggestion, she nodded. Abigail noted that the Queen appeared to have rested little. She was glad that she had given a helpful solution to her.

Dressed and ready for her meeting, the Queen hoped that her sluggishness would not interfere. Since their last meeting together, Ashor had seemed hesitant to speak his mind. She felt relieved that he had initiated this appointment. She did deeply appreciate him. He had a calm, yet firm way about him that conveyed to others that everything would be fine. For many years, they had labored together and enjoyed a flourishing Sheba. Over the years, he had become almost like a father figure to her.

He stood when she entered the room, and they greeted each other as they had so many times before.

"What news of Sheba do you bring me today?" she asked.

"I must admit," he replied, "we have met more times than I care to remember to discuss issues of this country we both love." Nervously, he continued, "I know that you are busy, but I must, for my own peace of mind, speak to you. I fear that I owe you an apology. Now that I understand more of your fervent desire for this journey, I feel that I let you down to initially respond to you so negatively. Since you were a young girl, I have only wanted the best for you."

The Queen swiftly spoke up, "My friend, Ashor, of all my leaders, you are the last one whose motives I would question. I know of your care for me, and I will always cherish you for it."

Surprised by her emotional response, she stopped her conversation abruptly. Yes, her words were true, yet seldom were their discussions so personal. She saw the look of relief on his face.

Momentarily embarrassed by her endearing words to him, she simultaneously knew the answer to yet another question. She startled herself at how quickly she blurted out her thoughts. "Ashor, would you be in charge of Sheba for me while I am away?"

Obviously taken by surprise, he seemed to be processing her request, since so quickly their conversation had changed from one subject to another. "Excuse me, did I hear you ask me to govern Sheba in your absence?"

"That's exactly what I said," she reiterated. It was crystal clear to her. He was the perfect one for the task. He was familiar with all the national issues, steady, and loyal. Yes, she was thrilled with her decision.

With reddened face, he spoke, "My lady, you never cease to surprise me! I have come to the palace to offer apologies and suddenly find myself temporarily elevated to the most honored position in all of Sheba. No one can take your place, but I will wholeheartedly devote myself in all ways to this appointment."

She had not expected this matter to be settled so easily. They nodded and smiled. "Set aside your afternoons for us to meet."

"Yes, Your Highness," Ashor spoke as they left the room together. It had been another brief meeting with the Queen, yet the implications were enormous.

Gratitude for such a noble man flooded her heart. As she made her way through the palace halls, she acknowledged to herself that she had, despite her sleepless night, managed to complete the highest priority on her list. She was fully satisfied with her decision.

12

Word was sent throughout Sheba that the Queen would address her people. She had the reputation of one who excelled in public relations and international diplomacy. Having ruled since age fifteen, her abilities and skills had matured well for such occasions as this. On that day, many had gathered in the city square, and the Queen began her eloquent address.

"Sheba is blessed with power and riches. We reach to excel in all goodness. We seek for truth and excellence. I have heard of a nation that has the distinction of excelling in wisdom. The king is said to have accrued great fame for the knowledge and depth of wisdom he has obtained. That nation is Israel, and their ruler is Solomon, king of the Jews.

"Perhaps many of you have heard these reports. I have gathered all the information possible. I have searched for the meaning of it all. If this news is indeed true, then we as citizens of Sheba must know the certainty of it. If Solomon is as wise as they say, then I must honor him and hearken to the words of his mouth that we may learn from his great utterances.

"Perhaps you have learned of the people and kings who have already traveled there to see firsthand if the reports can be confirmed. I am convinced that I must join the entourage of monarchs who visit Jerusalem on behalf of their people, their respected nations. This is the desire of my heart. I go on your behalf to

Jerusalem and will retrieve whatever riches of wisdom I can for all of Sheba. I will be your representative, and I will bring you the reports from afar."

As the speech drew to an end, the Queen announced with pride that Ashor would be in charge during her absence. The whole of Sheba knew him to be a wise and virtuous man.

Her speech was responded to with loud cheers and vigorous applause, for many Shebeans had heard of Solomon and his kingdom. Their curiosity fueled their passionate response and eager anticipation of a firsthand evaluation from their Queen.

All across Sheba, an unanimous voice of the people arose in support of the decision their monarch had made. Her strength of character and resolve was again displayed for all to see. They believed in her judgments and were proud of her. Joining their hearts with hers, they felt as though they also traveled alongside her to share in this noble quest.

Traveling back to the palace, the Queen basked in the warmth of the enthusiastic response of her people. She was truly blessed to be the leader of a nation of citizens who respected her regard for wisdom and demonstrated their devotion to her.

She arrived home in her extravagant palanquin after making her path through adoring, cheering Shebeans. Assisted from the mobile four-poster bed, she stepped to the ground. Abigail, who had missed their leisurely moments together, met her with a welcoming smile.

The recent events had kept the Queen much busier than usual. Meetings, meetings, and more meetings had become the norm. Already informed of the Queen's intentions to travel to Jerusalem, Abigail did not know if she was happy or sad about the news.

The Queen breathed a sigh of relief, knowing that the most important aspects of her preparations were completed. "Abigail, would you join me for a light meal in the courtyard? Let's take a few minutes to catch our breath together."

"Certainly," she replied. "I will join you as soon as I notify the kitchen staff." Relieved for a chance to be with the Queen, she quickly returned, eager to hear what they might discuss. Entering the courtyard, she hastened to retrieve the Queen's cloak. Already she felt the refreshing breezes and sat down for a cup of tea with her gracious leader.

As customary, the Queen initiated conversation. "I see the inquisitive look on your face. I wanted to be the one to tell you first of my plans. As you know, my time of late has left little space open in my schedule. I have had much business at hand, but you must know that I would not dream of making this journey without you by my side. You are my closest confidant. I want you to come with me."

The clear night above them revealed the fresh stars appearing in the sky. In this setting, the quiet was soothing and perfect for relaxing.

When Abigail hesitated to respond, the Queen continued, "You know that all you need will be provided. We will have many, many days of travel to visit and enjoy each other's company. Your companionship will be as a rock to me. And of course, your beloved husband, Timothy, will accompany us. I would not want to be without his protective oversight."

It seemed that the more the Queen spoke, the more difficult it became for her to interpret the look on Abigail's face. If she did not know better, she was certain she saw sadness. But that made no sense. She knew Abigail loved her company.

"Abigail, are you all right? You know that you can tell me anything."

Abigail looked down, taking a deep breath. When she refocused her gaze on the Queen, a single tear fell from her eye. She began to explain with her softly spoken words. "My lady, I am with child."

Their eyes locked, and instantly, the Queen knew she would have to go without Abigail. So new was the thought that she was temporarily speechless. They both understood the risks involved for a woman who was with child. She could not endanger the life of Abigail or the gift within her womb.

The sadness settled upon them both. The food before them was becoming cold. The Queen reached out and placed her hand on Abigail's. "I am truly pleased for you. This child will bring you and Timothy great joy." Determined to make the most of what time they had together, they began to eat.

The Queen, realizing the isolation of her position, heartily regretted that her most familiar friend would not be able to experience this quest with her. Momentarily, she wondered if she could go without her. Who would she have to share this journey? No one was as close to her as Abigail. Perhaps she could wait and travel after the birth, yet she knew such thoughts were selfish. She must collect herself and look forward to sharing every detail of the journey with Abigail when she returned.

13

Later that evening, Abigail reflected upon her earlier conversation with the Queen. She was accustomed to sharing more of the monarch's life than anyone else and was having difficultly making sense of her heart's dilemma. She and Timothy had wanted a child for years. In fact, so many years had passed that they had accepted that a child might not be in their future— ever. When she realized after the passing of months that she was pregnant, they felt this was the most perfect gift they could ever receive. They were favored to live in the palace and come under the wings of a benevolent queen whom they both loved and admired. Every need for them and their child would be richly provided. They also were confident Abigail's work would not be hindered by this birth. The child would have the devotion of all the palace servants.

The Queen had vowed to never lose Abigail as her personal assistant. Abigail had seen the changes in her Queen of late. She could barely keep up with all the developments. She had to embrace this reality that she would not be there to witness and share the profound experiences awaiting the Queen. She vehemently did not want to let go; she wanted to be beside Her Lady always. The struggle she felt was draining away her strength.

How could two of the most monumental events of her life coincide? Why was it impossible to embrace both? She had never traveled outside of the Shebean territories. And with this failed opportunity, she probably never would. How could she be consoled? As one dream came true, another perished.

Startled by the hand of her husband on her shoulder, she looked up into his eyes. Seeing his kind countenance, she began to weep. Timothy embraced her in silence.

Once Abigail could cry no more, he tried to reassure her. "As you know, we cannot always see the whole picture. We must trust there is a purpose in this. Our child may have a destiny that will influence the future of Sheba. Even palace servants can play a part in the future of a nation."

Abigail was comforted by his lofty words. Somehow, speaking of their child made the reality of this blessing more vivid. She would hold an infant in her arms. She would raise a child in the luxury of a palace home. Surely, they had experienced a miracle in this long hoped for conception.

At least her separation from the Queen was only temporary. All would be well. Comforting thoughts found a place in her mind and her peace returned. She let go of her perceived loss, beginning to even see advantage in the situation.

The Queen would be gone at least a year, probably longer. By the time she returned, she would be adjusted to her new role as a mother. Then she would have the best of both worlds. How shortsighted she had been. She knew that this path was best.

"Abigail," her husband spoke, "the Queen has offered for me to be her personal guard to Jerusalem, if we like."

"What? Are you teasing me?" She had been so focused on her own disappointment that she had not listened to the possibility of Timothy going. Dizzy in her thoughts, she exclaimed, "Of course, of course, we would like this."

She was consoled. This was perfect. A part of her would be with the Queen. And Timothy could tell her about everything when he returned. But what about the months of her pregnancy? She would have to give birth without him by her side.

"The decision is yours," he spoke.

Abigail hesitated, then continued, "The palace servants are our family. As much as I want you both places, I feel you must go. It will make my joy complete to know you are with our Queen."

She rested her head upon Timothy's shoulder. The stillness of the night settled upon the palace as Abigail drifted off to sleep. With the morning would come a replenished servant, refreshed from a day of emotional complexities.

14

Intent on doing everything possible to help prepare for the journey, Abigail was at the Queen's side as much as possible. She pushed herself even harder, as though to compensate for their upcoming separation. Dinner had just been finished when they heard a knock at the door. The palace guard shortly arrived with a sealed envelope that had been delivered from Uncle Hanam's courier. He placed it on the table before the Queen. The color drained from her cheeks as she looked upon the parcel. She asked for another cup of tea and reached for the unopened letter. Pale and emotionless, she read the note. Scribbled awkwardly upon the page were the words, "You shall go to Jerusalem. You shall die. I shall rule." The note was signed, Uncle Hanam.

The Queen felt numb. Why should she be tormented by him? Truly, this was one of the strangest circumstances she had ever experienced. She knew she could not let his words penetrate her mind. However, the implications of his deranged thinking convinced her that she had to take action.

"Abigail, I know it is late, but you must at once send for Ashor. And please take this note and hide it in my personal belongings where no one can find it. We have to make some emergency plans to enforce in my absence from Sheba. Have Ashor brought as soon as possible to the palace."

"Yes, Your Majesty," spoke Abigail, feeling ever so uneasy.

The Queen was still in the dining room when Ashor arrived. She did not want to have the conversation that would follow, but knew she must. She discussed the threats made by Uncle Hanam, and together, they examined what plans should be put in place to ensure that nothing could ever come from his deranged ideas. She had never appreciated Ashor more than she did in this moment.

Abigail and the Queen sat down together, enjoying a cup of tea. They had an important decision to make together. Someone had to replace Abigail on the trip.

"Abigail, I have not worried about this decision in the least. I trust your recommendation completely."

"I have thought long and hard, my lady, about the best person to travel with you. I have surprised myself by my choice. Increasingly, I have become focused on Marion, the woman who directs the care of Uncle Hanam.

"From all reports, she has done a fine job running his household. She is strong and hardy, which should be beneficial in the desert climate. I have met with her mother, who has diligently worked by her side and feel that she is qualified to replace Marion at the ancestral home while you are away.

"Marion is a very practical type of lady and will take her service to you seriously. Her father's side of the family has been involved at the Temple Awwam, with her great-great-grandfather actually being a temple priest. They are all faithful servants."

The Queen was quiet a moment, then answered, "If you feel she is the best choice, then it shall be. Prepare her for her duties, and I will not give it another thought."

"Very well, my lady," replied Abigail.

Meetings with Ashor, meetings with Tamrin, and brief, quiet reprieves with Abigail at her side, this was the Queen's life until finally the day approached. The palace staff braced themselves for the departure of their Queen. Would she return safely? Would Sheba remain strong without her? What would the months ahead entail? The uncertainty of the unknown produced a sense of vulnerability in the hearts of the servants.

Because of Sheba's isolation, the country had been secure from military invasion for at least 500 years. Shebeans appreciated that they were independent and at peace with their neighbors. This was a great consolation to them. They could surely withstand this temporary absence of their Queen.

"Abigail," the Queen spoke, "I have reassured Ashor that you will be available to him for help in all palace matters as you have been for me. Knowing that you continue your duties for him as he leads will be a constant source of reassurance to me. No one understands the workings of the palace better than you. I have told him to trust your insight if he has questions.

"I have also commanded him that you are to have as much time and rest as you need in the coming months. After listening to me, he most likely will see to it that you are quite spoiled while I am away. You must give birth to a healthy baby, the newest member of our palace family. He understands and will provide you with whatever you need."

The Queen encouraged an early dismissal for Abigail, so that she could have the entire evening with Timothy. Tomorrow was the day that a new chapter would begin for the country of Sheba. They would depart early for a full day's journey.

15

The Queen's mind felt foggy when she was jolted awake by the sounds of heightened activity within the palace. She was served tea, but then she was abruptly inundated with servants doing every imaginable task, all needed to bring together a successful launching. Her mind transitioned into a very business-like mode needed to approach her day. A surreal anticipation of what was ahead began to explode in her heart. Was she actually going to embark upon this revolutionary pursuit that had reeled in her imagination for what seemed like ages? She tried to ease her anxiousness by reminding herself of Tamrin's superb qualifications to oversee the caravan.

Tamrin had advised her that their caravan would consist of hundreds of camels laden with provisions and gifts for Solomon. Her mind wandered as she considered the massive amounts of food and supplies needed for the many months of travel ahead. She was grateful that the camels could carry much weight. The servants continued to complete the preparations. The Queen remained pensive, as though mentally preparing herself for the assignment at hand. Having dealt with her Uncle Hanam's threat, she truly was on her way to Jerusalem to live, not to die.

Never had such a vast entourage journeyed from the palace grounds. "It is time," came the familiar voice of Abigail. Simultaneously, all the other attendants vacated the room.

Abigail's visible sadness was noticed by the Queen. No doubt, Abigail had already gathered all of her strength to part with her precious Timothy, father of the unborn child within her. Now, in the silence that engulfed them, Abigail's eyes expressed tenderly her affections for the Queen. There were no words to describe the bond between them. Their absolute trust, love, and loyalty to each other calmed the apprehensions they each felt. Grasping each other's hands, they headed for the door.

"My lady," began Abigail. "I prepared a note for you. Someday on your journey, you may want to hear the words of a familiar friend. I have placed it in your parcel of personal items. Daily, when I think of you, I will lay my hand upon my necklace and utter a prayer to the gods for you."

"I am not surprised that you think of ways to strengthen me, even in my absence," replied the Queen. "You are a precious gift."

Abigail walked closely by the Queen's side as they made their way to the palace doors, this time the scene of a royal exit, not to be reentered by the Queen until many moons over a year. Awaiting was Timothy to assist her onto her extravagant gold palanquin, the richly cushioned four-poster bed that would transport her. There was a roof to shield her from the sun and draperies she could close for privacy. Her handsome white camel was draped with gold chains and emblems to win the favor of the gods. She would be accompanied by Timothy to protect her each step of the way.

The Queen approached the palanquin and observed the far-stretching view of camels that were strung together by ropes made of goat hair. She stopped and turned, facing the palace where she had been Queen since she was fifteen years of age. Memories flooded her mind of her mother, Queen Ismenie, and her father, chief minister to Za Sebado.

She then peered upon her servants who would stay behind. Splendid and loyal subjects looked upon her, their faces revealing both sadness at her departure and deep pride for her gallant quest. She gathered her courage. Her course was set. She had made her decision and would not turn back. Head held high, shoulders back, she made her way into the palanquin with the gracious dignity she was known to possess.

What she was not prepared to view was the multitude of Shebeans who lined the Incense Road while they crisscrossed their way out of the city. As the irrigation systems and high dams which contributed to the growth of the highly prized spices became visible, the waving and cheering countrymen and women began to disappear. Her aspirations were no longer a dream. This new reality was quickly becoming her life as she entered into the unknowns that awaited.

16

Two Months Later

The howls of the desert winds were deafening. The caravan had set up camp earlier than usual for the skies forewarned of the possibility of a tempestuous night. The Queen was not prepared for what she saw when she peeked from the safe enclosure of her tent flap. The hurling sands etched an unspeakable motion of gray chaos descending upon the vast stretch of tents, their home away from home. She could not possibly sleep during such a raging storm. So many people surrounded her, each surviving the intensity of the night in their assigned tents, strategically arranged to protect the caravan from the fervor of the desert sandstorm. On the other side of the curtain were her attendants, with the tents of her guards nestled around like bees surrounding their hive.

In the howling, the hurling, and the raging winds, she had never felt so alone. Though surrounded by endless tents occupied by her traveling family, isolation engulfed her. Her handmaidens waited in silence. *At least they had each other*, the Queen thought to herself, as she lay alone and gathered up the quilts close to her neck.

The night seemed endless. The tempest without created a tempest within as they all nervously awaited the momentum of the storm to wane. The danger they faced was all too real. The thought, "God, keep us all alive, please keep us all alive," played over and over in her mind. She did not know which god she beckoned, but calling out to a god was the only thing she knew to do. Minutes seemed like hours, and hours seemed like days as she wondered if the violent storm would ever end. The suffocating anxiety overwhelmed her, and she fell under the spell of total exhaustion.

As morning dawned, her limp body felt heavy. She attempted to move. Aware of her thirst and parched lips, she roused herself and tried to think clearly. Out of her daze, she began recollecting the events leading up to the present.

The Queen had no idea how much time had lapsed. The quietness was unsettling. With the sun up, there should be much activity. Something was wrong. She began to hear faint muffled sounds of life from far away. She called for Marion and felt relief when she heard a reply. The Queen pushed the ornate curtain to the side.

"This is no time for formalities. What do you know? How have we survived the dark night? Where is Tamrin? Where is Timothy?"

By the overwhelmed face staring back at her, she knew she must calm down.

"My lady, Timothy is anxious to speak with you when you are ready," Marion responded, quite frankly not appreciating the Queen's barrage of questions. After all, her night had been terrorizing as well. "We have not wanted to disturb your needed rest. Apparently, the storm left a thick blanket of sand upon the whole camp. Some places are having to be dug out. Let me give you a drink of water and help you freshen up for the day."

Just hearing Marion mention Timothy somehow comforted the Queen. How quickly the spirit that was in Abigail seemed to be present with her husband as well. His presence had the ability to reassure her. She gladly drank from the reserves of water and was totally surprised when hot tea arrived for her. Perhaps some sense of normalcy might return to them after all. Amazed at how much activity could occur in such a confined space, the Queen was finally prepared for the meeting.

She was startled to see Timothy in such disarray. Coated in white dust with black circles around his eyes and extreme tiredness in his voice, he greeted her. She feared for his collapse. He must have read her mind.

"Do not be afraid, my lady. I will be fine after I recuperate from the long evening. We are done accounting for everyone. All have survived, but not so among the herds. We fought hard for many hours to protect the goats from the storm, but after the first few hours, it was obvious that we would only be able to save the ones that could be put in tents. We realized that we risked our own lives to continue attempting to protect them. It is too early to tell how much our milk and meat supplies have been affected. We did bring extra animals, since we anticipated dangers along the way. The camels' hardiness has served them well. As of our last check, we have lost none. Tamrin continues to oversee the work of digging away the remaining walls of sand so that we can continue the journey as soon as possible. He asked that I report to him of your condition."

She looked down in silence, thankful for the champions who accompanied her. She reeled within at the real danger they had all survived. Stoically, she responded, "Tell him I am well. Thank him for his sacrifices."

In her numbness, she moved aside a strand of hair from her face, then placed her hand on Timothy's shoulder and dismissed him by her words, "May you long be blessed for your bravery."

Alone, she recalled the days and days of monotonous travel. But in this moment, she wished for the return of the mundane. The consolation of knowing that no one was lost to the storm helped her recover from the initial feelings of devastation. They would recover, and the caravan could soon resume.

The Queen was confined within her tent by the mountains of sand, as if she were a common prisoner. She did not even open her tent flap for a breath of fresh air because the dust was still stirred up from the storm. She lay down for what seemed to her like hours and began to feel a slight chill as she reached for the quilt. Alarmed by the ache in her head and the churning of her stomach, she wondered if the stress of the storm was having a toll on her. Suddenly, she began to shiver. By the time Marion responded to her call, she was shivering uncontrollably.

"Marion, have someone bring my physician. I fear that I have become ill."

"Yes, my lady." She hurried to send for help.

Returning quickly, she saw before her a very pale queen, violently shaking and holding her stomach.

"I am so sick," uttered the Queen as she lay on her side curled up in agony.

Marion grabbed what she could to prepare for what seemed like the inevitable. The Queen began to violently vomit, purging the contents of her stomach until she had no more strength. She continued heaving, her stomach desperately attempting to eject its contents, although there was nothing left in it.

Marion struggled to know what to do. Though she was a large and physically strong woman, she realized the Queen needed more than she could give her. She was relieved when finally the physician arrived.

Immediately concerned by what he saw, he began forcefully giving orders, "Fetch some lukewarm water and clean cloths, bring more attendants to help, send for Timothy."

Marion felt bombarded. She returned with other attendants. The physician placed one in charge of dealing with the continued regurgitation and two in charge of bathing the Queen with the lukewarm cloths. The last attendant he told to make sure every spot of residue from the Queen's sickness was cleaned up.

"What has the Queen eaten today?" the physician asked Marion with alarm.

"Why, she has only had water and hot tea. She has had nothing to eat."

"Where is Timothy, what is taking him so long?" the physician questioned in a stern voice.

Timothy was out of breath when he arrived.

The physician stepped outside the tent, but his loud voice could still be heard. "I believe that the Queen has drunk some contaminated water. She has all the symptoms. You must immediately send out a team to inspect every water container in the camp. There may be others who have drunk from the same supply. This is urgent, perhaps a matter of life or death. Send out another team to stop all drinking of water until we have found the origin of the toxic supply."

Marion and the other handmaidens stayed by the Queen's side. Her stubborn fever persisted, but finally her vomiting subsided. Marion was certain that she heard someone whisper outside the tent that another person had fallen ill. She and the other attendants were exhausted. They had just bathed the Queen with the lukewarm cloths again.

The physician spoke to them, "We have done all we can for now. Her chills have eased a bit. Let's begin to sit with her in shifts. Continue the routine. I will rest in a tent next to hers and check on her regularly. Call if there is any change. Marion, you take the first shift. The Queen is most familiar with you. Less activity in the tent may help her rest."

Left alone with the Queen, Marion was uneasy about all that had happened. Although she knew she had done nothing wrong, it troubled her that she had served the water that may have caused all of this in the first place.

While Marion sat in quiet, the Queen stirred and slightly opened her eyes. She spoke in a barely audible voice, "Please, please get me the sealed letter within the parcel of my personal items. Please read to me the words from Abigail."

Marion knew, as did everyone else, how close the Queen was to Abigail. Yet it seemed strange to her that as frail and weak as the Queen had become, that she would make such a request.

Marion reached for the bag and felt inside it to retrieve the sealed note. She opened it, and as the Queen looked her way, she gasped as she read, "You shall go to Jerusalem. You shall die. I shall rule, signed Uncle Hanam."

Marion felt the dark cloud of doom descend upon them. What had she done? This could not have been the letter sent by Abigail. Could she not do anything right for the Queen? She was confused and afraid.

The Queen faded into a state of mental confusion. Marion could not understand her ramblings.

Frantically, Marion began to search the parcel where she had found the note. She thought that she would panic. Finally, she found another piece of folded parchment. This must have been the note the Queen wanted her to read. She opened it as quickly as she could.

"My lady, my lady, here is the note you wanted me to read," but the Queen did not respond. "Do not worry, I shall read it to you another time," she spoke in defeat, placing the letter back in the parcel.

The next shift of help approached the tent. They took one look at Marion and hoped that she would go to bed. She had a ghastly look of weariness upon her face.

Several days passed. The Queen continued to recover from her sickness. She had vague recollections of someone holding up her head for sips of water and strange dreams interrupted by damp cloths wiped across her forehead. Today, as she awoke inside the tent, she was hungry. Seated nearby, resting, was Marion.

"Marion," came the first word from the Queen in days.

"Yes, my lady."

The Queen looked perplexed. "I can't remember what has happened. Please send for Tamrin and have some food brought to me."

Marion left, relieved that the Queen was alert and hungry, both good signs.

At last, Tamrin stood at the entrance of her tent. He looked at the Queen, and a feeling of great relief filled his heart.

"You gave us quite a scare," he began.

"Please tell me what has happened," she urged, not even caring that she lay totally unprepared for a visitor. "I remember the sandstorm, but nothing since then."

"You have been very sick. We feared for your life. During the storm, one of our containers holding water was overturned by the strong winds. The lid was ajar. Sand, as well as several dead lizards, were found in the contaminated water. A servant set the jar upright, not realizing what had happened, and several people of our caravan consumed portions. All of you have fortunately survived, except for one of our servants who tended to the camels. The physicians feel that he may have already been weak because he was older, and he did not recover."

The Queen blankly stared at him. Her face was thin, her eyes hollow, her body frail from days of no food and little water.

Tamrin continued in his forthright manner, "The servants have arrived with something for you to eat. Please consume what you can. You need to regain your strength." He bowed and left the tent.

Marion placed the nourishment beside her bed.

The Queen wondered if she should have ever left Sheba to take the journey. The urgency of the quest that led up to this day somehow felt far away. In fact, it was alarming that all of her motivation was clearly dissipated.

"Marion, would you read to me the note from Abigail? It is in my satchel of personal belongings."

Would she! She had been waiting for this moment. Apparently, the Queen did not remember what had happened. This time, she retrieved the correct letter. Opening the note, she began to read, "My lady, I know that you have made the right decision. I shall lay my hand upon the necklace each day and pray to the gods for you. You will return to us in great peace. Abigail."

Marion felt as though she witnessed a miracle. Almost instantly some color returned to Her Majesty's cheeks. The power of the words to strengthen the Queen was unmistakable. She was thankful for the recovery she saw taking place but somehow resented the way hearing from Abigail gave life to the Queen. She still felt guilty that she had given her the toxic water.

The Queen of Sheba was ready to eat. But more importantly, she was also ready to refocus her thoughts, so that her inner fortitude would not unravel. She must think about why she was here in the first place. Where was the original allure now, she wondered, feeling alone in her unfamiliar surroundings. Her desire to experience the fame of Solomon and his God seemed like a lofty idea and somehow hollow, but she decided she must focus her attention on the day she would actually arrive in the foreign country for which they were enduring such dangers.

"My lady," interrupted Marion, "you must eat."

The Queen sipped her soup, determined to finish it. She appeared to be in deep thought. *This was a good sign that she was improving*, thought Marion.

Completing her meal, the Queen revisited in her mind her earlier thoughts. What would she say when she first encountered the king? Would she reveal the inward pursuits of her soul to him? Would she tell him why it was that she risked everything to come to Jerusalem? She decided to carefully consider each question she would address in Solomon's presence. How much time would he devote to her? If she only had a brief audience with the king, then she must make sure she spent the time discussing the matters that were most important to her. Solomon's renown for wisdom caused her to want to discuss the issues that were most urgent and significant to her. Would she test him with hard riddles? Would she pour out her heart and reveal to him her deepest longings? Could she trust him to be a safe haven for her heart? She somberly considered all these things as she faced yet another day of desert sojourning. With each new day of travel, this must be the focus that she would maintain, so that on the day she met Solomon face-to-face, she would be thoroughly prepared. She fell into another deep but restful sleep.

17

The sea of endless days engulfed the Queen with their suffocating powers. Now additional months had passed since the caravan left behind the scenes of sand rubble. Each day resembled the last, and their fortitude was tested by the monotonous passing of each sunset. Long gone were the romantic notions that originally motivated this pursuit. The Queen was plagued with guilt when she considered the plight she had plunged so many of her servants into by bringing them with her.

She desperately missed Abigail. How easy it was to take for granted someone who knew you almost as well as you knew yourself. That kind of rare companionship was a treasure to find, especially by royalty, who were often socially isolated from the people they governed. Having Timothy along was a close reminder of the unselfish love that Abigail held for her. Abigail's life would have been easier with her husband by her side throughout the pregnancy, yet Abigail sacrificed him to bridge the gap between her heart and the Queen's.

Briefly, the Queen wondered if she would ever have a "Timothy" in her life, someone with whom she could share the richness of life that he and Abigail displayed so well. In Sheba, she never had time to entertain such thoughts. But now she had more time than she wanted even as Sheba seemed farther away than she could have ever imagined.

Another sunset passed, and the massive expanse of tents, animals, and people encamped for another night in the desert. The tasks needed to enter into the evening routine were completed. The group was like a traveling city, packing up each morning and unpacking each evening. Day after day, this had become the habit of their unending travel. Once they were settled at the end of each day, the quiet of the desert became disrupted only by the noises of animals mingled with soft chatter.

The Queen had enjoyed this evening more than most. She actually reclined around the fire with some of her attendants and enjoyed stories about Sheba. They shared laughter and conversation in such a casual manner that she almost felt as if she were one of them and not the revered Queen who was to be approached with formalities and ritual. She liked these times, which had begun to happen on a more regular basis. Such endearing moments had filled many personal needs she had felt for warmth and companionship. It was nice to relax and feel more like a comrade than a ruler, if only for a brief time. After the last sip of tea, the Queen dismissed herself and left to ready herself for another desert night's sleep. With the help of Marion, she completed her personal agenda and made her way into her sleeping quarters.

She laid her head upon the feather pillow and appreciated the peacefulness of the night. She wondered how many more evenings it would be before they would actually arrive in Jerusalem. Surely they were closer than they knew.

Suddenly, like the clashing of men at war, came loud screams and movements that she had no framework of understanding. In all these months, she had never heard these peculiar sounds. What could cause such commotion? As the whole camp was jolted awake, the Queen's attendants scurried around her, and the royal guards surrounded the tent, determined that no harm would come to their Queen. What could be happening?

The shrill noises continued and a rumble of activity could be heard throughout the camp. The raging of battle and corresponding cries blew over the encampment of Shebeans. It seemed to go on forever. Finally, a wave of silence fell upon them. All remained quiet, as they hoped for clues of what was happening. They longed for the interpretation. Something was really wrong; this they knew. What would be the outcome of this strange frightening night? They waited, waited and waited for word…nothing. What did the silence mean?

Immersed in the petrifying quiet, the Queen remembered the apprehension of her beloved Ashor concerning the trip. Was he correct? Had she endangered all of their lives? Was her cause worthy of the sacrifices that had been already made? Resisting the terror of these thoughts, she attempted to steady herself. The enfolding events could not possibly be as horrible as the doom she felt.

An hour must have passed. She was accustomed to displaying a calm and reassuring demeanor under stress, but she was certain her attendants could see through her present facade. But none of this mattered. What mattered was that no one be found harmed—no one.

At last, she was asked to come out of her chamber, where she was met by Tamrin. Not knowing what to expect him to say to her, she braced herself. He began a detailed report of what had happened.

"My Queen, we have been attacked by a band of thieves. They must have spied on us for some time and determined the location of the gold and spices. After they believed us to be well into the evening routine, they began their advance, making their way toward the hidden treasures. They slipped through our first lines of defense unnoticed, drawing closer to the guarded riches. It was here that most of the fighting began. By this time, Timothy, hearing the commotion, secured multiple guards for you and made his way into the chaos, arriving just in time to witness one of our guards about to be stabbed. Throwing himself between the knife and the guard, Timothy struggled to save him. The bandit fought hard, but Timothy overcame him at last.

"It was not until the thief breathed his last breath that we realized Timothy had sustained a wound in his shoulder. When the thieves saw that one of their own was dead, they quickly began to retreat. While they made their way back through the outer banks of the camp, many were killed. We have lost no one, thanks to Timothy. We have lost no treasure in human life or royal riches. Truly, Timothy saved the life of one of our most skilled guards.

"It was then that we realized the knife was still implanted in Timothy's shoulder. We brought the physicians to him and carefully they removed the weapon. They wait by his side to see how he endures the night."

The Queen had no words to respond. She felt dizzy and faint. Nothing could have prepared her for this news. Trying hard to maintain outward composure, her paleness and unresponsiveness signaled to the attendants to help her. They must move quickly, or soon, she would pass out. They gently laid the Queen upon the cushions, reaching for wet rags to lay on her forehead. With a fixed gaze, the Queen allowed them to help her. She felt so helpless and vulnerable in full view of those who served her.

Emotional intensity paralyzed her. She closed her eyes as though to protect herself from those staring at her, while they tried desperately to bring her out of this overwhelmed state. She was numb throughout the night. Lifeless she lay, eventually falling asleep. The Queen did not move until the normal rustling sounds of the new day awakened her.

The morning seemed routine. How could there be calm so quickly? She listened to the surrounding noises, seeking for reassurance that normality really had returned; whatever normal was during these months of endless travel.

She replayed in her mind the happenings of the prior evening. Could it be that the life of her dear Abigail's husband was in the balance? She could not bear to think of this possibility. How could she look Abigail in the eyes and tell her that her beloved husband was dead? No, she could not think like this. She wondered what had happened to the Queen who somehow remained optimistic under the most dreadful circumstances.

Now she waited, vulnerable, weak, and all too aware of her human frailties. She began to cry. Her nomad world had drained the life from within her. Where was the adventuresome spirit she once knew when she was eager to seek the truth, no matter where that led her? The confusion and heaviness that she felt slowly lifted with the falling of each tear. She struggled to regain her composure and take her focus off her own pain. The intense compulsion to find out how Timothy was recovering began to overshadow her own conflicts. And with this thought, she arose, anxious to prepare for the day and resolute to see him.

Dressed and determined to hear the voice of Abigail's husband, she made her way out of the tent, rushing along, pursuing the location of Timothy. The attendants could hardly keep up with the Queen, and the guards tried not to seem startled by her sudden unannounced activity.

"Where is he?" she asked, heading in the direction she felt he would most likely be. Hardly pausing for an answer, she continued darting toward the area occupied by the Shebean physicians.

"My lady," came a voice from behind. "Tamrin left us instructions early this morning where you would find Timothy. If you would do us the honor of slowing down a bit, we will lead you there."

Approaching the tent, she paused and attempted to gather up her strength. The guards saw her, and one of them disappeared into the tent to announce the arrival of the Queen. Not even slowing down to greet the outer guard, she pushed aside the drapes of the tent entrance. After briefly signaling the others to stay back, she alone entered.

There he lay. Steadfast were his eyes as he looked up into the Queen's face. She quickly tried to process everything she saw in order to interpret his state. She immediately noticed bruising on his face, no doubt from the struggle. The bandage in clear sight was soaked throughout with fresh blood. Dried blood was caked in his hair. Yet his eyes were clear, strong-looking in spite of the story told by the rest of his exposed body.

"I will be fine," he spoke with determination, attempting to eradicate her fears. "I will quickly recover and be as good as new."

The courage that Timothy displayed after battle was no less than the courage he showed during it. She stared at him. *What a noble man*, she thought. A true champion was in their midst. Was he not the most deserving one to be in charge of her safety? Humbled to be served by such a man, she turned and commanded that the keeper of the royal books come quickly and prepare to write an official proclamation for her to make in the presence of her surrounding retinue.

A flurry of activity occurred in order to fulfill the Queen's orders. Everyone waited outside the tent for the scribe to arrive. No one heard the conversation between the Queen and Timothy. They left them alone for a private privileged conversation that only the two of them would hear.

Hastily, the scribe and his attendants arrived. The Queen pushed pack the curtains of the tent and with great authority began to address all those who had gathered outside. Timothy could be seen as he lay upon his bed behind her.

"In my servant, Timothy," she began, "I have witnessed the sacrificial spirit of a true champion. He is indeed of pure and righteous character and shows unending love for his country and those he serves. I decree that from this day forward, throughout the duration of Sheba, his family and his blood descendants will always be promised a position in the royal palace. Such a regal spirit must find its home among royalty. This proclamation, I, Queen of Sheba, make in the presence of my fellow countrymen. His lineage will always be honored by the sovereigns who rule over the territories of Sheba. I make this solemn vow and decree that it be honored by all rulers who follow me."

18

Not much time had passed since the Queen had returned to her tent. What an exhausting day so far. She was about to indulge in an afternoon of rest when Marion approached.

"My lady," she spoke as she bowed, "I am to give you a message from Tamrin."

"Certainly," came the quick reply.

Marion continued, "One of our scouts has returned. Tamrin felt that you would want to know we are approaching Moab and should arrive in a day or two. He requests a brief meeting with you before entering the new region. He also has decided not to break camp since the dark will soon be approaching, and he bids you rest in preparation for an early morning departure."

"Yes, of course, tell him that I am thankful for the report," came the hoarse reply of the tired Queen.

Having seen the face of Timothy, she felt some relief settle upon her spirit. His countenance was that of a strong and determined man, and she felt reassured that he would survive. The fact that Moab was nearby signaled that the desert travel was about to end. No longer would they be isolated from familiar sights and villages, perhaps not unlike ones in Sheba. Could it be that this would be the longed-for turning point in their journey? The sojourners would welcome an end to their desert travels and its grip upon them. The departure of the uncertainties, uneasiness, and harshness experienced would not be missed. Reassured by the encouraging news, she reclined for a much-needed rest.

How long had she slept, she wondered, as she turned in her bed. The fragrance of fresh bread awoke her, and she was surprised at how motivated she felt to start the day. Then she remembered, she did not even awaken for supper the night before. No wonder she was starving. Reaching for the bell, she rang for Marion.

With her first uttered words, she inquired about Timothy. Satisfied that he endured the night well and was much improved, she thoroughly enjoyed the warm bread and hot tea. It seemed to her that the whole camp awoke early. She supposed that everyone was ready to leave behind the dusty desert, and head for new terrain. And that they did. Leaving the campsite earlier than usual, the vast caravan began edging toward new horizons. She hoped that with each passing hour, they would be closer to a change of scenery. For the past five months, no matter how often she peered out through the curtains of her traveling home, the landscape had always looked the same.

The sun was setting, and the Queen was asked to join Tamrin for dinner. Accepting the invitation, she anticipated what he might want to discuss. Anxious to hear again of Timothy's condition, she made her way with several attendants to the evening meal. The tent curtains were opened for her as they arrived, and she was welcomed inside.

Bowing, Tamrin greeted the Queen. The table was already prepared, and they reclined to enjoy the meal. Her eyes focused upon the food before them. She was shocked at what she saw, yet a smile of approval quickly appeared on her face.

"Fish, my dear Tamrin, however is this possible?" Months of desert travel had caused this delicious entree to be a distant memory. Obviously delighted, she eagerly awaited his response.

Tamrin began to speak, "The king of Moab is aware of your journey and has offered gifts, the fresh fish being only a sampling. He has freely given us ample supplies for the rest of the journey to Jerusalem. He has also offered some of his personal guides to assist us on the most convenient route to Jerusalem, if you so choose. Please eat, my lady," he spoke, anticipating her excitement to consume some of her favorite foods.

And eat she did. Fish had never tasted so good. The simple dish was more flavorful in this moment than the richest palace delicacies. She had almost forgotten the lavish royal meals of old, being afraid to remember, lest she regret their absence too deeply.

As she consumed the carefully prepared meal, she asked Tamrin, "Please report to me of Timothy's condition."

"He is recovering as valiantly as he entered the fight. In fact, the knife wound is healing well with the help of some of our balm of myrrh. There is no more bleeding. He already wants to resume his responsibilities, the only delay is hearing your approval. He is strong and eager to report for duty. The physicians are amazed. Forgive me, I must let you enjoy your dinner."

He could not believe how much he had spoken. His face reddened as he realized that the Queen had finished her main course. Her plate was bare and his full. He also noticed the Queen's demeanor. Color had returned to her cheeks. The good report and excellent food must have worked their magic in her.

"Please relay to Timothy that I request he rest until we arrive outside Jerusalem. I need him to regain his strength fully, so that he can be by my side when we enter the city," she replied. Then, satisfied to turn to another subject, she began, "Tell me, what have the scouts to report of their interactions with the Moab people?"

Having had a moment to catch his breath, Tamrin replied, "Well, as you can imagine, the news of your travel here has caused much conjecture. Everyone is aware of Sheba's reputation, and they are intrigued with the stories of our wealth, thriving agriculture, and beautiful gardens. They all wonder what you look like and believe you must be very beautiful, to be Queen over such an affluent and powerful country."

At this, the Queen blushed. How amusing to imagine that the Moab people would be intrigued this way with her. Trying quickly to change the subject, she asked, "Why do they say I have come?"

Without even a moment's hesitation, he replied, "They assume that a Queen, such as yourself, has surely come to visit Solomon to set up trade agreements and conduct business contracts."

As fresh fruit arrived, Tamrin's statement began to impact her. She was surprised at how caught off-guard she was by his words. Trade agreements? Business transactions? Whatever were they thinking? Those kinds of interactions were not totally improbable, or were they? Such motivations had been completely overshadowed by her intuitive quest to experience the wisdom of Solomon and his God. She tried to process the report.

Baffled and a little amused, she finally responded, "Indeed, these curiosities and assumptions, I find interesting and shall have to ponder."

"Well, forgive my bluntness, but isn't this the reason you are here, my lady?"

With a strange look in her eye, she simply said, "We shall see…"

For a moment, Tamrin felt the awkwardness fall upon them as they finished their meal together. He sometimes felt that he did not totally understand the Queen. What was the meaning of her words, those of this woman he intensely admired, revered, and sometimes found to be a mystery? He decided it best to drop the subject and instead ended the meal with small talk that did not feel uncomfortable to him. The two of them talked throughout the evening and enjoyed themselves, anticipating in the near future the end of their trip to Jerusalem.

How quickly the evening passed, the Queen thought to herself. It was odd, but of all that they discussed, what remained in her thoughts were Tamrin's remarks about the purpose of their trip and how surprised she was by his focus on trade agreements and the like. Lying on her bed, she knew that what gripped her heart during this unlikely journey was something she would truly have struggled to articulate to him. How would she have explained the private inspiration that took her heart by force and spun her into such an intense quest?

The Queen remembered a prior conversation of how "the fame of Solomon and the name of his God had spread throughout the whole earth." She contemplated the words again. This phrase, "name of his God," was a new way to reference gods. She understood that "name" denoted the character and personality of a person. What were the traits of Jehovah? Her gods, labeled as the god of agriculture or the like, were easily understood by their titles, but not so much known by personal characteristics. She wanted to know the descriptions for this Jewish deity.

Drawn by the mysterious depiction of a presence that could be cherished or the traits of a person that could be known, she was mystified. If Tamrin could perceive her thoughts, how shocked he might be at how opposite they were to his assumptions.

19

Two Weeks Later

The royal couriers transported messages back and forth between Jerusalem and the Shebean caravan. Solomon was anticipating in advance the long-awaited arrival of this impressive entourage delivering their royal monarch.

There was much interest surrounding her arrival. The Israelites had never known the sole leadership of a queen. Only led by kings, the citizens of Jerusalem and Solomon were filled with curiosity. Speculations abounded. The caravan continued toward the gates of Jerusalem. Tamrin was constantly replying to requests from Solomon as to how the Israelites might best prepare for all of their needs when they arrived.

With each passing day, the caravan was met by more welcoming bystanders who had heard of their approach. The Queen was well-hidden from sight, situated in the center of this vast traveling village. Surrounded by guards and comrades, she attentively listened to reports as she looked forward to the moment they would reach their destination.

Any day now, they would enter the gates of Jerusalem. The details of their arrival were being well-planned. The practical arrangements, as well as plans for an entrance fit for a queen, were being completed. Finally, as the sun set and the last encampment was completed, all in this enduring caravan knew that tomorrow would be the beginning of a new era and a much-needed reprieve from travel. The excitement mounted as they anticipated the welcome that awaited them.

That night, lying on her bed, the Queen pulled back her tent curtains. Glistening darts of light from the full moon graced her chamber with their whimsical movements. Never had her palace walls allowed these frolicking flickers access to entertain her. In the isolation of her desert experience, moments such as this had been the joys that carried her through the everyday difficulties. She watched the dancing rays and began to prepare herself for the changes which were imminent.

Many months had passed since she had been in the public eye. In fact, this solitary season had been quite new to her. She wondered if she was ready to be thrust into the spotlight of the curious citizens of Jerusalem. She was grateful for the full force of attendants who would help her to be outwardly ready. But only she could prepare herself mentally. Ready or not, tomorrow, she would be arrayed with all of the pomp and lavishness of the queen of an affluent country. However, her aspirations were still to leave Jerusalem filled with more treasure inwardly than she displayed outwardly. With that last thought, she drifted off to sleep.

The awakening sounds of the morning increased with intensity each passing minute. She heard her attendants rustling around much more hastily than normal. Even after she received her tea and honey cakes, their activity never changed pace. Quietly, she ate and drank and listened to the whirlwind of soft chatter outside her drapes.

"It is time to prepare," spoke Marion to the Queen. Her voice sounded deliberately subdued as she tried to maintain a peaceful atmosphere. Marion felt stressed by the storm of requirements needed to make the Queen ready.

"Come in," replied the Queen. "Whatever we need to do, I am ready." This moment, after all the months of anticipation, felt unreal as she placed her cup beside her bed.

It seemed like a lifetime since the Queen had been arrayed in her bejeweled attire and dazzling robes. The attendants skillfully prepared her for a magnificent presentation, sure to impress the impending audience. They had received word that Solomon had made ready a luxurious apartment in a palace close to his official residence for his royal visitor and also lodging for all who accompanied her. His thousands of stalls for his horses and chariots would be the new home of all the animals and equipment brought from Sheba.

She heard the voice of Tamrin explaining the strategy for their next maneuver. The Queen's palanquin had to be transported from its position of obscurity to the site of greatest prominence before the approach into Jerusalem could begin. The morning was still early. They were on schedule to arrive and be met by King Solomon himself.

Eventually, the palanquin was perfectly relocated with only a small surrounding of guards. Strategically placed, the Queen of Sheba would be able to view her new surroundings and to be easily seen wherever she passed. Embraced as a royal guest, she was assured of safety and invited to enjoy all that was a part of this great kingdom. After making sure the Queen was comfortably situated upon the cushions, her closest attendants slipped outside to walk beside her to provide for any need that might arise.

She peered through the beautifully woven curtains and could now see the massive stones of the wall surrounding this city on a hill. Just outside the gate, they awaited final word to proceed. At last, Timothy addressed her through the drapes. She immediately pushed aside the tapestries to behold his bright face. He looked so proud of this moment. Fully recovered from his injury, Timothy was obviously elated. The first part of his mission was accomplished. The Queen had safely arrived, and now they were about to experience the fruit of their traveling labors.

He was beaming as he spoke, "We are ready. Do we have your permission to begin?"

"Absolutely!" she said with a smile upon her face. Finally, the time she had dreamed of was unfolding.

With great honor, Timothy tied back the lavish materials that enclosed the Queen. Now she must be on display for all to see. She was dressed in some of her most royal attire. Golden and white were the colors of her gown draped by a luxurious woven robe which was embellished with beads and jewels. The entire bodice was overlaid with gold beadwork. White layers of silk chiffon fell to the ground with golden threads forming exquisitely embroidered patterns at the base of her gown.

Her crown was gleaming with a row of dangling jewels falling upon her forehead. Her braids, woven with golden stones, coiled elegantly behind her head. She displayed the extraordinary elegance that only could be conveyed by a queen.

The Queen heard Tamrin shouting orders. They began to move, followed by long lines of camels and dromedaries, heavy-laden with supplies and gifts. Entering the gates, they could see the nearby tented markets, where people were buying and selling goods from what seemed every corner of the Near East. Resting near the wells were caravans that appeared to be from Syria and Egypt. Emerging from the midst of Jerusalem could be seen hundreds of one- and two-story mud-brick houses, narrow streets, and busy bazaars.

Word spread ahead of them, and faces turned in their direction. Welcoming cries and smiling citizens met the Queen's reciprocal glances as her approving welcome spread among the people like a wave rippling upon the sea. There was a genuine excitement blended with warmth exuding from the inhabitants of Jerusalem.

How kind and endearing the people seemed to be. Some waved, some applauded, but all smiled upon her as the royal entourage traveled through the streets. She was enchanted by the smiles embracing her as she passed.

Suddenly, in the distance, she heard the cheering of crowds. She saw whirls of dust ahead. Emerging from the thick clouds came a chariot surrounded by what appeared to be bodyguards. *That must be the King,* she thought to herself. *That must be Solomon!*

The caravan was coming to a standstill. She watched and was quiet as he approached. Escorted by many guards, he emerged, a dark-haired figure with a complexion bronzed by the sun. He was a tall man with a commanding presence. His arms and legs were muscular. Abounding in vitality, he was full of joy and vigor. His dark striking eyes seemed to look into her very soul. Decked in elegant tunics and golden collars, he addressed her with a gracious smile. With all of the charm of courtly manners, he spoke, "Welcome, honored guest. All of Israel's blessings are your blessings. Our goodness is your goodness. Come share in the splendor of our nation."

Their eyes locked, and the Queen drew from deep within to respond with eloquence to his words, "It is with great joy that I accept your invitation to share in the treasures and accomplishments of your great kingdom. May all of Sheba be enriched by your hospitality."

Solomon continued, "Some of my choice guards shall accompany you to your prepared apartment, close to the palace. I trust that you shall find the arrangements we have made most pleasing. Take time to be refreshed. Would you do me the honor of joining me tomorrow for touring, followed by a banquet at my palace in the evening?"

"Of course," she replied, "it would be my pleasure."

Upon Solomon's face emerged a smile. For a moment, he seemed to study her face. He then nodded and returned to his chariot.

Her heart was racing. What an impression he made upon her. She was not quite prepared for such a handsome King who carried himself with rich authority and grace. He spoke with uninhibited enthusiasm. As she traveled the rest of the way toward her apartment, she could not stop thinking of the grandness of his stature.

The caravan resumed its way through the winding streets of the Jewish inhabitants. Peace abounded throughout this dominion, which extended from sea to sea. Parts of the city seemed to be decorated just for their arrival. Some citizens had bouquets of flowers which they delicately tossed in her direction, with each fragrant blossom falling one by one. Basking in the warmth of her gracious and kind reception, the Queen enjoyed the last moments of their approach to this mystifying new home away from home. She felt in a daze.

They stopped at the entrance of their apartment, an architectural splendor, where they were met by friendly servants focused on making the transition flawless. Assisted down from the familiar palanquin and escorted into her new lavish dwelling, she was greeted with fruits, flowering trees, silks, linens, tapestries, and exquisite garments, according to the Israelite customs. She was informed that her staff would be given meat of oxen, bulls, sheep, goats, deer, cows, gazelles, and chicken for their meals each day. In addition, they would receive wine, honey, fried locust, and rich sweets. Perhaps the best surprise was the singing men and women given for their enjoyment while in Jerusalem. She was utterly astonished by the overwhelming generosity and kind reception.

Proceeding to her sleeping chamber, she soaked in the foreign curiosities as she saw the imported playful apes and colorful peacocks sunning their magnificent plumage about the courts by the garden fountains. Amazed at all that she witnessed, she was ushered at last into the room that would be her private refuge, her secluded fortress for contemplation of all that her heart had to process.

20

The Shebean team began the tedious job of unpacking and settling into their new habitat. Now that they had arrived, a meeting with Tamrin would be in order, so he was invited to join the Queen for dinner in the evening. For now, she chose to have a light meal in her room and rest for the remainder of the afternoon. The relief she felt at the culmination of their travels left her even more aware of how exhausted she had become the past months.

Marion completed unpacking the final personal items of the Queen as another attendant brushed her hair. The evening supper would be more casual than most.

"My lady, I feel that you look as though a burden has been lifted from your shoulders," spoke Marion, promptly blushing as she wondered if her comment was awkward. "I mean to say that you look very refreshed and not as though you have just completed a long, wearisome journey."

The Queen was puzzled at times by how uncomfortable she felt around Marion. But she was far, far from home and could do nothing about it without causing quite a stir. So she tried to accept the reality and ignore her feelings.

The caravan experience had seemed much more informal than life at home in the Marib palace. *They must adapt to the return of a bit more formal orientation*, the Queen thought as she simply replied, "Thank you, I feel rested."

The table was set and dinner was about to be served for the evening. Stationed outside of the dining room was Timothy. Already, it was hardly noticeable that he had sustained an injury just weeks earlier. The picture of health, he had fully resumed his role of assuring the safety of the Queen.

Tamrin and the Queen were seated across from each other at the table. As the food was served, the conversation began.

"Tamrin, I must thank you for a job well done in achieving a successful trip here. You have performed your duties brilliantly. My appreciation of you has intensified for all of the caravans you have led for Sheba over the years."

"The gods have blessed us to arrive safely with only one casualty. I am as pleased as you," he replied.

Smiling, she continued, "What do you think of the legends about the power Solomon has acquired from his devotion to his mysterious deity?"

"That you will have to ask Solomon for yourself. Perhaps, though, your purposes would be better served if you began on a lighter note with him." Tamrin always seemed confident in his opinions, the Queen observed.

"Tamrin," she continued. "Since you have traveled extensively all these years, I would love to entreat your thoughts as I contemplate how to best engage this King in conversation tomorrow at the banquet."

"My lady, as you know, the wit and wisdom of the East to a large extent is enshrined in proverbs and tested by riddles. It is sport for dignitaries to hold contests of riddles, much like our experience. Like you, they find it very entertaining." replied Tamrin. "Begin with riddles for small talk with the King."

"So he would not be offended by this?" questioned the Queen.

"Not at all, he would find it charming." All of Tamrin's travels must have served him well. He seemed to have good intuition at knowing what would fit into the culture of his host.

"Would you help me with the preparations?" she asked.

"Of course," he replied.

They discussed at length what riddles they might bring before the King, hoping to brighten his day by this amusing activity.

"It is said that Solomon has written thousands of proverbs and hundreds of psalms," spoke Tamrin. "According to the Jewish scrolls, he speaks about plants, from the cedars in Lebanon to the hyssop growing on the wall, also of animals, birds, reptiles, and fish. The King is known to gather about him the wonders of nature, drawing from them the secrets of their existence."

"Really!" the Queen answered as though surprised. "I expected his wisdom to be political and theological in nature, but I can't say that I anticipated him to be a natural history expert. How far-reaching is his wisdom, like the grains of sand along the sea, it would seem."

"I must admit that I have been continually impressed by each new report that has come across my path," Tamrin concluded.

There was a pause in their conversation, and then they realized that they had finished their meal. They sat quietly, satisfied not only by the food, but also the hearty exchange of ideas and information.

"Should we not retire for the night?" came the request of the Queen, as though speaking with a friend.

The comment, perfectly placed in the evening, brought an enthusiastic, "Yes, my lady," from Tamrin.

Retiring to their individual new residences, each welcomed the arrival of the sweet dew of sleep. The morrow would beckon with an entire day of new experiences.

21

The howling of the wind and bright rays of the sun joined to awaken the Queen from her slumber. Even before her fragrant tea arrived, she arose and crossed the room to the window. Her chamber, high on a hill, allowed her a tantalizing view of the city.

Jerusalem was bustling with activity. Markets were preparing to open. She observed the inhabitants from afar; whether citizen or visitor, she knew not, but they all seemed to be beneath the spell of this famed city. In her mind, she imagined what the goods for sale might be, horses from Anatolia or copper from Cyprus. Within the tented markets, she pictured fine cloth from Egypt and ointments from Syria. Such goods were in demand in Sheba and other Arabian countries.

Although the King and Queen had met briefly, today would be her official welcome in the palace. She needed to be dressed yet again in her most prized royal garments. Her attendants assisted her with all the preparations. At last, the details had been completed. Today, she was dressed in luxurious royal purple colors. Her most exquisite crown, gleaming with precious stones, was placed upon her head.

She was greeted outside her room by Timothy. His presence was a catalyst once again for her thoughts to return to Abigail, whose friendship she dearly missed. And as they had hoped, the accompaniment of Abigail's beloved Timothy was the bridge that eased their separation. He led the way through the corridor and outside to the palanquin. The accompanying entourage began their transporting of the Queen to the King's royal residence.

They approached the compound, the King's ornate palace rising before them. It was built on a high ridge overlooking Jerusalem. They had been told that the Phoenician-styled palace was built of wood from the Forest of Lebanon. Also resting upon the hill was the rectangular stone temple built for Jehovah. This massive structure, as well as the palace, had been constructed with the help of Phoenician architects and laborers.

Having arrived and dismounted for their stay, they were led by one of the King's servants through the long Hall of Pillars to the throne room in what was called the Hall of Judgment. There, seated on a high gleaming chair overlaid with gold, surrounded by scribes, attendants, and officers, sat Solomon. Suddenly came the realization that she, the Queen of Sheba, who had traveled with one goal in mind, was actually, finally there in the presence of the King of Israel. He was surrounded by all of the lavishness of his great kingdom.

He greeted her with royal charm, pomp, and ceremony. Her eyes met his, and she instantly wanted to dive into the questions held in her heart. After their exchange of greetings, the King himself offered to take her on a tour of his palace and surrounding gardens. She responded with a hearty acceptance of his offer. The two monarchs thus began crossing the bridges to build a new friendship and strengthen the ties between their two countries.

The King smiled and offered her his arm to begin the tour. He was pleasant as he spoke. "Your country has captured my imagination. I have heard of Sheba's beauty and admirable qualities. I enjoy hearing about your peaceful nation whose citizens enjoy its abundance."

"We have been blessed," replied the Queen. "King Solomon, your kingdom has a lavish display of opulence, yet the spirits of your people are even more astonishing to me. What is their secret?"

They walked along the garden path beside a stream as he replied, "Their secret is wisdom. Happy is the person who gains understanding. The proceeds of wisdom are better than silver or gold."

The King was a gracious and vivacious host, thought the Queen while they continued their walk. She liked his answer. He had a sincere and earnest manner about him.

The Queen was beginning to feel a bit drained by the heat of the sun, when Solomon made a suggestion.

"Let's stop for a moment in the shade of a tree," he spoke.

Just ahead of them was a large beautiful fig tree beside the stream.

"Look," said the King, "the figs are ripe. You must try one!"

Like an exuberant child, he hurried to pick some of the choice fruit. Then, he turned to the Queen and gave her the best figs.

She took her first bite and closed her eyes as she enjoyed the robust flavor.

"They are so succulent," spoke the Queen.

As they enjoyed the sweetness of the figs, Solomon began to speak, "Blessed is the man who delights in wisdom. He is like this tree planted beside the water. He will bring forth fruit in season as this fig tree. His leaf shall not wither and whatever he does shall prosper."

The Queen finished eating. The joy she received from the delectable fruit accentuated the descriptive words of Solomon. He was just like she had imagined him to be. He possessed the skill of taking the simplest ordinary truths of nature and depicting extraordinary life lessons in a way that anyone could understand clearly. She had heard a saying that a man's wisdom caused his face to shine. Indeed, she observed a brightness about Solomon's countenance, a handsome one at that!

The Queen enjoyed the magnificent vineyards, gardens, and pools of water as they returned to the palace. The conversation continued to flow effortlessly between the King and Queen.

Solomon's palace was bathed in splendor and luxury. There were singers and musicians with exotic musical instruments made of ivory, gold, and sandalwood. They walked beside the draperies of crimson and purple and her eyes feasted upon the breathtaking architecture. The Queen had grown up engulfed in the richness of palace life with the grandness of it etched within her. Yet as she observed the surroundings of this magnificent home of Solomon, there seemed to be a distinctive quality present. If she was correct, she felt that the joy displayed and the peace exhibited surpassed the idyllic picture in her mind of Sheba. She did not know how to respond to this notion. She wanted to be open and objective, yet curiously felt a twinge of national pride rising inside, loyalty to her country gripping her.

The King seemed less complicated than she thought he would be. A startling clarity effortlessly guided his words, seemingly painting each uttered phrase with a positive stroke of optimism. Stability in his thinking was apparent as he interacted with his guest and staff. He was obviously a capable administrator.

She was exhausted by the touring, hampered by her inactivity during so many months of travel. Hoping to be revived by dinner, she was relieved when the banquet was ready, and they were seated for an evening of royal entertainment. Dish after dish of palace delicacies were served. Although seated near to the King, she was thankful for the exuberance of the hall musicians and ongoing activity. They allowed her to eat in peace and quietly digest both food and thought.

She had never even imagined such wondrous music. What was it about the quality? She felt somewhat inebriated by the mysterious effect the melodies had upon her. No anxious thought could survive within the intoxicating notes. How comfortable she felt! How at ease the music made her feel! She could quickly adjust to this tranquil sea of peace that engulfed her. On and on the evening continued, until at last she and Tamrin were invited into the courtyard for a more intimate interaction with the King.

She felt she should be nervous. This was the part that had been arranged between the staffs. They would share some riddles. But how could anyone feel stressed after total immersion in such a bath of peace? To the contrary, she found herself intensely enthusiastic about the amusement to follow.

Tamrin had worked hard to prepare for the theatrics of the riddle they had chosen together to begin the marvelous evening of mental gymnastics. The Queen had entertained so many questions for the King. She wanted to bring to him philosophical questions and challenge him with assortments of riddles. And now, at this moment, she was about to launch into these unknown waters of discovery. She noticed that her heart pounded as her anticipation grew.

Her thoughts were interrupted by the entrance of the King. She wondered if she was blushing as she effortlessly went through the less formal greetings shared between these two influential monarchs. The atmosphere pleasantly engulfed them while they spoke of the evening and all of its pleasures. The King engaged her in questions about her country. Before she knew it, she was endlessly speaking of Sheba and all that she loved most about it. He welcomed her detailed depictions of the life and culture of her kingdom, as she charmed him with her deep love for the citizens who made her country grand. She was enjoying this opportunity to share her life with someone who listened so attentively.

Solomon was intrigued by this woman as he listened to her descriptions of life in her nation. Never had he heard a female so impassioned for the people over which she ruled. In fact, he had never met a "she" monarch at all! As he looked at her and pondered her, he realized that she was a novelty to behold, bold in her presentation and rare in her depth of purpose; he was admittedly mesmerized.

Just as the King's royal visitor was winding down her narrative, Solomon's servant approached and whispered in his ear. With a nod, the King smiled at his guests and graciously thanked the Queen for her personal introduction into the intricacies of life in Sheba. It was time to commence the amusements planned for the evening.

Solomon looked at the Queen, and with a twinkle in his eye, he welcomed her to begin the activities with her first riddle for him. Accustomed to the staunch competition of men with strong egos, he was secretly amused as he anticipated what this beautiful woman had planned for his first challenge.

Tamrin rose and escorted before the King five youths dressed identically. They bowed and stood at attention before the King.

Eager to test Solomon's ingenuity, she presented the riddle to him. "Now, before you stand these five children. Would you give us the honor of trying to detect which are girls and which are boys?"

Solomon spoke into his attendant's ear and without a moment's hesitation was brought five bowls of water, which were placed before the youngsters.

With absolute gaiety, the King spoke to the children, "Now wash your hands before us."

One by one, the King pointed out which were the girls and which were the boys.

"Why, you are absolutely correct," spoke the Queen. "Now tell us how you knew."

With the quickness of an eagle, he answered, "When the children washed their hands, the girls, unlike the boys, rolled up their sleeves! That is how I discerned the difference."

"Marvelous!" exclaimed the Queen, as she clasped her hands together in glee. She continued to the next riddles. Oh, how they laughed together. This was proving to be exhilarating, until she realized that it was her turn to respond to his chosen riddle.

The King gave a brief introduction. "I have chosen to have reenacted a real-life riddle that I was forced to judge." Gesturing for his actresses to come in, the Queen was immediately surprised to see two damsels and a baby brought before them. She had no idea what to expect next.

Solomon began to tell his story, "As a young King, I was brought two women who had become mothers out of wedlock. The first woman to speak explained that the two of them dwelt in one house, and each had delivered a child. She complained that the second woman's child had died and this woman had taken her own newborn, replacing him with the deceased baby in her bosom as she slept. Both women vehemently argued that the one surviving son belonged to them! So the riddle presented to you is how could one discern which woman was telling the truth?"

The Queen's mind was churning while she attempted to maintain her composure. Indeed, this situation was complicated. Her first impulse was to assume that lengthy interrogations were pursued with neighbors, family, and friends to get to the bottom of this mystery. Knowing that this kind of investigation would take many days or even weeks, she hoped for direction by posing a question to the King.

"Your Majesty, might I ask how long it took you to arrive at your answer?"

"Why, only a brief moment," he responded.

The King rested his elbow upon the arm of his chair and placed his chin upon his hand. He appeared to move forward in his seat, as though his curiosity was building in anticipation of the Queen's answer.

The Queen felt an intense surge of competition rising within her. He would not get the better of her. Shocked by his answer, she began her analysis. Striving to respond quickly, she reviewed the possible alternatives. Well, he must have threatened the women in such a way as to provoke the truth out of them. Certainly that was the answer. Why, he must have decreed death to the mother who was lying, intimidating the deceiver to confess. With that thought, she knew she had to present her answer in a wise way, so that she would have carved out ample space to be right! She had to give the correct answer. She refused to fail in front of this great King.

"Your Majesty," she began, "I believe that to understand the truth, you must have made a decree so stunning, so threatening to the deepest recesses of their hearts, that they had no recourse, but were forced to reveal their true motives."

There, she had said it. Her heart was pounding, yet she sat in silence awaiting the King's reply.

The King's hesitation emphasized the hush that fell upon the room. Truly stunned by the Queen's correct deduction, he attempted to poise himself as he decided how to proceed. This Queen from Sheba certainly had a brilliant mind. Far be it from him not to give credit when it was deserved.

Surprised by his excitement at her correct answer, he exclaimed, "Noble guest from Sheba, you have pinpointed my precise strategy. Like an arrow thrust from a royal bow, you have struck the eye of the target! Indeed, I commanded that a sword be brought to me and the baby be cut in half!"

Was she hearing correctly? She reeled with shock and confusion. Was her answer really correct? Was she wrong? What, he commanded that a baby be cut in half? Why, her mind could have never conceived of such a plan. Even as she debated with herself, the King continued his story.

"In response to my command, one of the women began pleading for the infant's life, willing to give the child to the other if need be to save the life of her offspring. In that moment, the true mother was revealed. I had no doubts."

The Queen began to accept his reasoning. What she had said was the same, was it not? Her words flashed through her mind, slowly releasing her from the anxiety flooding her emotions. Yes, this was a command that cut through to the core of maternal hearts, unveiling the truth in a moment. Never would she divulge that the decree the king had made was starkly different from any scenario she could have imagined. However vastly different their approaches were, yet the same!

She had upheld her dignity. The King was visibly impressed by her answer. However, deep down, it was the Queen who was held in awe of his wisdom. Never had she heard of justice being brought in such an impressive manner. His wisdom was certainly distinguished from any other she had ever known. Was it any surprise that it was said that all of Israel stood in awe of the King when they saw and heard the wisdom of God in him to do justice?

22

The Queen awoke early and reflected on the prior evening. She had relationships with men in Sheba; however, most all of them were concerned with the running of the nation and commerce. She could not remember a time she just simply enjoyed an evening with someone like she had last night! Expecting her time with Solomon to be serious, sorting out all of the issues pertaining to life, she certainly had not anticipated joy and sport to define her early interactions with him. She could get accustomed to such gaiety. Just to enjoy the presence of a man, now that was a novel thought.

For a moment, she considered the culture of the East, in which a man having many wives and concubines was common and considered a status symbol. Women often seemed thankful just to have a husband who provided for them. She could not relate to that thought. Never would she marry a man unless she were certain that she would enjoy a relationship defined by companionship, love, and mutual respect.

Unbeknownst to the Queen, Solomon also awoke early in his palace. This winsome and quite beautiful monarch from Sheba was the focus of his thoughts. The Queen was very mysterious to him. She possessed so many qualities that he admired. Her love of country and seeking heart set her apart as a rare woman indeed. He felt that her motivations were pure in coming to Jerusalem. She certainly did not come with idle curiosity or to only pursue business opportunities, for she herself possessed abundant riches and wealth. Obviously, she had no intentions of becoming his wife, for her ardent love of Sheba was obvious. Unlike other wives, who would be content to live in the shadow of their husbands, this monarch was a different creature altogether.

He was fascinated by her mind. He had observed the beauty of many females, but had not, up to this time, felt the enticement of a woman who possessed such a brilliant and inquisitive mind. This was new territory for the King. He had never known the friendship of a woman he could relate to so easily. They were compatible in many, many ways.

At that moment, he startled himself at how lost he was becoming in his own thoughts. Intentionally, he began to remind himself that he could never find satisfying companionship in one who served false gods, for he was educated about the deities of Sheba. He tried to end his obsessive thoughts about the Queen. After all, she was only another visitor who had come to see if the reports of his kingdom were true.

Even though the King had managed to stop his reflections on the Queen, that did not alter the fact that they were scheduled to spend time together again today. He sincerely wanted to share his kingdom with her, and he wondered at the possibilities of sharing his God as well, in due time. He knew it would be impossible for her to get to know him without coming face-to-face with the One who had blessed Israel with all the lavish goodness surrounding them. His desire was that every visitor to Jerusalem, no matter what country from which they originated, would return to their home believing that there was one true God in heaven.

23

The evening skies in Jerusalem were magnificent. Star-speckled magic lit up the darkness; draped with mystical hues of soft colors, the clouds faded in and out of sight. All of the Queen's senses had been deliciously fed this day. Her eyes had feasted on gardens of rare flowers. Her taste buds had discovered foods oozing with new flavor combinations, which she consumed with great pleasure. The attractions unique to the bustling capital city satisfied her longing for adventure. Now, she was about to complete her day with yet another anticipated delight, spending time with the King.

The courtyard of the palace provided a welcoming atmosphere, much more casual than the night before when pomp and ceremony dominated the scene. This evening, Tamrin was spending time with some of Solomon's leaders. She and the King could talk privately. Yesterday, the Queen might not have been prepared in her heart for time alone with the King. But tonight was different. She was ready.

"King Solomon, tell me, how is it that you have become a man famous for the wisdom he possesses?" She waited for his answer, already captivated by his warmth and charm.

"You see, Queen of Sheba, I have not always been known as such a man. If you only could have been acquainted with me at the early age that I first became king, when I was but a lad, inexperienced and lacking in wisdom. Not yet recovered from my father's death, I was totally overwhelmed."

Her face softened as his words touched one of the most delicate places in her own heart.

"Were you twenty yet?" she asked.

"No, not even," he replied, taking note of her interest.

"I ached for my father," he continued. "No one truly understood my emptiness."

"Such pain can feel unbearable," she spoke softly.

They sat still in the cool breezes of the night.

The King looked at her curiously, "What is it I sense in you that makes me feel you genuinely understand my words?" he asked.

With tears in her eyes, she answered him, "I believe I do. My own mother died when I was very young. Father died when I was only fifteen, making me the official Queen with his last dying words. I don't think anyone who has not been in such a situation can comprehend it. I had never felt so alone and unprepared."

The King was visibly touched and leaned forward to wipe away her tear. Their bond was instant.

"Royal visitor of mine, thank you for sharing with me. The camaraderie I feel with you is rich and sure."

"King of Israel, I was expecting you to give me profound answers to my questions, and I am sure you will. Yet you have blessed me with the sweet gift of an understanding heart. For that I am grateful. We have much in common. So tell me, how is it that you have become the famed King you are known to be today?"

"As the young ruler I described to you, I did the only thing I knew to do. I loved the Lord and had gone to Gibeon to give offerings on the great high place. That night, the Lord appeared to me in a dream, saying, 'Ask what I shall give you.'

"It was then I called out to my God. I told Him my weaknesses and sense of inadequacy. I asked Him to give me wisdom to discern between good and bad. I desired from Him a heart to judge and rule well over His great people.

"God was pleased with my words and promised to grant me my requests. We spoke for a while, and then I awoke, realizing it was a dream. I was encouraged and believed what He told me."

"How gracious of your God to give you such an uplifting dream at a time when you needed support so badly," spoke the Queen. Looking away, she appeared troubled. "I had a dream as well on the night I became Queen."

"Indeed, we have much in common," said the King.

"Not so," she replied. "The dream was not as you might think."

The King was puzzled by her answer, but he did not probe.

"Well, my lady, only you know all that you have overcome to be the successful ruler of your powerful nation. You have done a wonderful job!"

She was stunned by his affirming words. They were life-giving to her.

"Your humility is remarkable," she spoke. "I have come to Jerusalem to learn from your great achievements and instead receive congratulations for my own." She blushed as she realized how honestly she spoke.

Solomon smiled, then continued, "There is gold and a multitude of pearls, but the lips of knowledge are a vase of preciousness. I only speak the truth about you."

She had never met a man who spoke so poetically. His words flowed forth effortlessly like a refreshing fountain.

Beneath the glistening stars, the Queen continued to ask the King more of the carefully chosen questions she had determined within her tent during the tedious travels there. One by one, she posed them with care to her gracious host. They were absolutely born from the depths of her searching heart, each one containing a part of who she was at her very core.

The King listened attentively. He displayed a genuine desire to please her. There were lengthy discussions between the two, and he comprehended easily the meaning of her questions. As each new subject arose, he answered her in a manner that brought satisfaction to her heart. There was nothing too difficult for the King that he could not explain to her.

Rumors had spread that the Queen was bringing hard questions to test the King. Surely, they would discuss issues related to death and immortality, peace and war and, of course, the meaning of life. Perhaps they would discuss political or economical issues. Certainly, she would seek astronomical knowledge from him because of his renown for developing a new calendar. The possibilities were endless. There, seated beneath the canopy of stars, only these two knew all that was said during their private conversation.

The Queen prepared for bed and continued to enjoy the satisfaction from her answered questions which felt like a refreshing dew. To her surprise, the answers from Solomon seemed to only make room for more questions. She had not anticipated that he would so freely give of his time to her. Never had she known someone who could answer questions in such a way as to totally satisfy the one posing them. It wasn't just that he addressed them, but his answers carried a peace with them as well. She was flooded with more questions, as though she were addicted to the medicinal qualities of peace and joy contained in his responses.

With each passing day, her interactions with the King grew more delightful. She was at ease and felt safe with him. The questions she was now posing had become extremely personal, yet she did not feel judged or uncomfortable. The weeks passed. Never growing tired of hearing his wisdom, she trusted in his words. The Queen was struck with the realization that with each encounter, she had communed with the King about all that was in her heart.

At times, she wondered what the meaning was of the mysterious feelings she encountered when she heard the wisdom of the King. His words were enveloped by an atmosphere that affected her in a very unusual way. How could she describe the way they made her feel? Perhaps she felt like an ointment had been poured upon her, soothing and healing as it flowed. Or possibly his responses were reassuring, whispering to her she would be safe and everything would be all right. She sought to describe how she was affected by his words, but truly could not identify the many ways. All she knew was that she felt wonderful and hoped life would never be normal again.

24

The Queen was still surprised by the deep friendship she had discovered with the King. For many years she had wondered if another person could ever feel as close to her as Abigail. And if such a person were to be a man, that would be even more of a novelty.

It was a beautiful day in Jerusalem. King Solomon was to accompany the Queen just outside of Jerusalem to Gibeon. He found the outing quite entertaining, especially as he watched the camels.

When the Queen gathered her gown to step onto the palanquin, the King noticed her slender feet within the jeweled leather sandals. Once they were seated, a mischievous look emerged on his face, and he could not contain his words.

"I was told, just before you arrived, the mysterious story of your feet being shaped like animal hooves."

Raising her eyebrows, the Queen responded, "Oh, and you only just now realized that the report is false?"

"Definitely not," the King answered, "that was one of the first facts I made certain. I did not want to open my heart to a beautiful woman with cloven feet and hairy legs!"

Pretending to be indignant, the Queen replied, "The rumors are not helped by the fact that my alabaster throne in Sheba is made with legs to resemble the hooves of a bull in honor of our chief god, Ilmaqah. When my gown drapes the feet of the throne, it is possible for onlookers to mistake the hooves of my throne for my feet."

The King smiled as he tried not to laugh. "Well, a good name is more important than even silver or gold, and that you have!"

With an amused look on her face, she asked, "Do you always tease your honored guests this way?" Then she burst out in unbridled laughter.

Pausing, she held forth one of her feet, her slender toes showing beneath the embellishment of the golden jewels on her sandals.

"Aren't these the most beautiful hooves you have ever seen?" she exclaimed.

They laughed until they could laugh no more.

Traveling toward Gibeon, the Queen suddenly remembered that this was the place the King was visited by Jehovah in the dream.

"King Solomon, how did you obtain the wisdom you requested from your God in the dream?"

"Early on I found out that the fear of the Lord is the beginning of wisdom." Quickly, the King saw the troubled look on the Queen's face when he uttered the word "fear."

She could not hold back the memories flooding her thoughts of her mother's fear of the gods as well as her own terrors of the night. "What do you mean by fear of the Lord?" she bluntly asked.

The King responded as he tried to understand her reaction. "Noble fear of our God is not oppressive. It is a reverential, worshipful honoring of our God, not to be confused with an unhealthy fear."

"Are you ever afraid of your God in a tormenting way?" she asked.

"Afraid?" he repeated. "I do not fear who He is. Can one be afraid of love? My God is love.

"Let me tell you a story. There was a time when the children of Israel traveled through the wilderness for many years. On their way, God Himself descended upon Mount Sinai, wrapping the mountain in smoke and fire as it shook. The people were told not to touch the mountain lest they die.

"The Israelites saw the thundering and lightning upon the smoking mountain and trembled with fear."

The Queen imagined what she heard. She could see the flames and lightning so vividly in her mind.

The King continued, "You can understand their concern when God told seventy of the elders and their leaders to come up to Him on the mountain to worship Him. Yet they obeyed God's instructions."

The Queen's mind was full of speculation. Would Jehovah demonstrate His powers so they would never forget Him? How would their supposedly all-powerful God manifest Himself to them? She was engrossed as she anticipated the rest of his narrative.

About that time, the camels carrying the palanquin came to a halt. They had reached Gibeon, and the servants brought out the most wonderful picnic to serve them. A beautifully woven tapestry was spread in front of the King and Queen as rich cheeses, unleavened bread, fruits, and wine were placed upon it. Then they were left to eat alone. The drapes had been opened so they could view the lovely countryside.

Politely, the Queen spoke, "The picnic is lovely, and I am reminded of the sacredness of hospitality it represents." She breathed a sigh of relief as her thoughts had turned from the intensity of the burning mountain to the comfort of breaking bread together. Remembering all that this moment of eating together represented brought her peace. The feelings of safety, kindness, enjoyment, rest, and so much more were wonderful to experience now in the midst of their conversation about fear.

"My King, I do not think I can eat a morsel until I hear the rest of the story."

"Then we shall finish it," replied the King. "You see, the elders proceeded to go up the mountain, although they could have been held back by fear. There, they saw their God, and under His feet was pavement of sapphire stone. God did not conceal Himself from them, nor did He harm them. But there they ate and drank."

"They what? They ate together?" the Queen repeated. She could hardly believe what she heard. The picture spoke volumes to her. Everyone of the East understood the meaning. The single scene spoke a thousand words to her. She felt wondrous joy. The King said no more. She was perfectly at peace with his poignant story as her fascination grew for the God of the Jews.

They began to eat together as Solomon poured the wine. Slyly, the Queen lifted her foot and wiggled her toes. The laughter erupted all over again.

Then, the Queen realized that the King may have seen the scar on her ankle. She felt very vulnerable in asking him the question that was on her mind.

"King Solomon, would a man be repulsed by a woman if she had a scar?"

The King got the most curious look on his face.

"What do you mean?" he asked.

"Very well, I will show you," lifting her foot to reveal the scar. "I was bitten by my pet jackal when I was a child."

"My dear Queen, a woman of your rare beauty need not fear the reproach of a small scar."

She blushed and was melted by his reassuring words. She could hardly believe she had asked him such a personal question.

The King looked at her kindly. *There would never be another like the Queen of Sheba*, he thought to himself.

25

Jerusalem was beginning to feel like the Queen's home away from home. All who journeyed there with her had experienced an extraordinary, peaceful way of life in this city far from Sheba. Marion told her some of the stories she had heard from one of the temple singers. The worshiper described to her how Israel had come to know peace from each and every enemy under Solomon's rule. Also, every single promise that had been spoken to them by their God had been fulfilled.

How absolutely amazing, the Queen thought. What a heritage, what a story the Israelites had to tell! No wonder the citizens of Jerusalem were such an exuberant people. They were the reason that the whole world knew of this place. Like candles put on candlesticks, they burned brightly to attest to the glorious life they shared.

Lying upon her bed, the Queen remembered an earlier conversation with Caleb about the uneducated cook from a ship in Israel's fleet. She thought about the dedication of the temple when Solomon prayed for the strangers who would come, realizing that she was one of them. The King had asked his God to hear the cry of the visitors and answer them, that they might know there was one God in heaven. She wondered if she should utter a prayer as well to see if this god would answer her in such a way that she might know whether or not he was the One True God.

On this fair morning, the Queen arose to greet a new day. Once again, she was invited to banquet at the King's palace that night. She would not be the guest of honor, but would be seated among the dignitaries who would be part of the celebration. Her afternoon was free.

Seated at her dressing table, the Queen signaled for Marion to come to her. Hastily, she stopped making the Queen's bed and came to her side.

"Do you know how to contact the temple singer who spoke with you?" asked the Queen.

"Why, yes. She lives close to here. We had such a wonderful visit together that she welcomed me to find her whenever I had free time and wanted the company of an Israelite friend."

"Splendid! Please go and see if she could visit with me this afternoon. We could have tea and nourishment in the courtyard."

"Yes, Your Majesty," replied Marion, slightly frustrated by having to leave her duties to fulfill this new request from the Queen. "I will give you her answer as soon as I return."

The warmth of the sun's rays greeted the Queen as she settled into her chair surrounded by the well-manicured gardens. She was excited that the young singer had been able to arrange a visit with her so quickly.

Bilhah entered the courtyard accompanied by Marion. She was introduced to the Queen and with a look of composure as well as curiosity, seated herself on the other side of a small table laden with teas and dainties. Friendly chatter filled the gardens as Bilhah was received as an honored guest.

They discussed the latest news in Jerusalem until the Queen guided the conversation to the main reason she wanted to meet the young woman.

"I suppose that you were present at the dedication of the temple," began the Queen.

A noticeable attentiveness came upon Bilhah's face. Her voice was impassioned as she answered, as though asked about her favorite subject. "Yes! Yes indeed! I was there."

The Queen continued, "I have heard some accounts about the dedication, and today, I would love to hear from you your favorite part of the festivities. What one part of the ceremony stands out to you above the rest?"

Without a moment's hesitation, Bilhah answered. Her voice became louder as she spoke, "When the glory and presence of the Lord filled the temple." Blushing because of her unanticipated passion, she wondered if she were allowed to say such a thing before the Queen of another nation who followed other gods.

"Please expound," came a hasty reply from the Queen, "tell me what happened."

Bilhah was thrilled to have been given permission to share this transformational moment in her life with the Queen. "You see, all of the singers and musicians were arrayed in fine linen. With cymbals, harps, and lyres, they stood at the east end of the altar, and with them 120 priests, blowing trumpets. We were joined in unison, making one sound to be heard, praising and thanking the Lord. I, along with the other singers, lifted up my voice, accompanied by the instruments. We could sing of nothing except the goodness of God and His mercy and loving-kindness, which endures forever, and then," she paused, "then the house of the Lord was filled with a cloud! And the priests all fell to their knees before the Lord because of the intensity of His presence, for His glory filled the temple."

Captured by the story, the Queen asked, "What happened next?"

Bilhah's face glowed as she continued to pour forth the fame of her God's goodness. "Let me see, how can I put this into words? When the cloud filled the temple, it was as though the atmosphere was heavy with an intense, pure, unfiltered revelation of love. I felt immersed in a sea of ecstasy, bathed in the warmth of God's love for me. Drinking the sweetest of wines would have paled in comparison to the infinite joy my soul encountered. I had no guilt, but felt pure like fresh-fallen snow and free like the wind. He opened my eyes to see His divine qualities, and I basked in the sweetest pleasure known to man. In those moments, I was able to see beyond my natural ability and watch as His explicit goodness passed before me.

"Please forgive me, I am a simple temple singer, I am not talented with words like an orator." Tears ran down her cheeks. "I only can attest that heaven came down that day, and a divine dew of revelation descended upon me like weights of bliss. It was impossible to stand. In that state, I saw our God more clearly than ever before. I was undone and fell prostrate on the ground. I became aware that none were standing, and I knew that my life would never be the same again. I only want more of Him."

The Queen was spellbound. She was lost in her thoughts.

"I want more of him," whispered the Queen under her breath.

"Excuse me, I could not hear what you said," replied Bilhah.

Hesitating and embarrassed by her words, the Queen changed them, "Well, I said I want more tea." She discretely wiped away a tear.

Bilhah was surprised at the Queen's sudden change of subject. But she also was astonished that she had actually been invited to share with a queen one of the supreme moments of her life. Just talking about that day allowed her to relive the most captivating moments she had ever experienced.

Bilhah realized that she and the Queen were sitting in silence. She really did not mind though. The sweetness enveloping them said everything. She did not know how much time had passed when they finally said their good-byes. But later that night, as she reflected upon her time in the garden, she uttered a simple prayer for the Queen, that she also would know the Presence of Jehovah similar to what had been experienced at the dedication of the temple. Little did she know that the Queen had prayed that exact prayer while alone in the quietness of the garden.

26

Seated at the palace dinner, the Queen was happy she was not the guest of honor. She preferred to be less conspicuous tonight as she sat between two dignitaries who were content with casual conversation. They did not seem to notice her sitting pensively while she observed all the activities taking place in the room. Having now gathered at this beautiful palace many times since her arrival, she immensely enjoyed each exquisite occasion. There was definitely a spirit of excellence about all that was accomplished in Solomon's kingdom. The palace itself was astonishing in all of its grandeur. The presentation of the savory entrees and rich dainties was indescribable.

Tonight, for some reason, she particularly noticed the Israelites who partook of this grand event. She studied the seating of Solomon's officials, the standing at attention of his servants, their apparel, then the King's cupbearers. There was a magnificence that thrived within this walled city. Could it be that the same presence described by Bilhah is what produced the extraordinary spirit even upon the servants and cupbearers? She pondered their faces. The joy she saw seemed genuine. Yes, they were happy, no matter what their position. In her world, she knew many noble yet empty people. What a contrast she observed between the two kingdoms.

Solomon had once again invited the Queen to join him after dinner. Because she always enjoyed her conversations with him, she hoped that her pensiveness tonight would not hinder the hearty exchange of ideas they typically shared. As soon as the last guests departed, he came to her and offered his hand.

"Come with me," he said with a twinkle in his eye. "I have a surprise for you in mind. The Jerusalem night is beautiful. Will you accept my offer to go on a stroll with me?"

This was a new idea, but she must admit, a walk sounded enchanting. Yet how would they work this out logistically?

Before she answered, the king had already anticipated her thoughts. "Don't be concerned, I have made all the arrangements for this to happen. I have already instructed Timothy and my personal guard to carry torches far enough away that we can speak privately and yet close enough to light our path."

The King had put a lot of thought into this idea, she noted. "And where shall we go?" asked the Queen.

"I have wanted for some time to take you to the temple porch on such a night as this. The walk from here is not as far as you might imagine. There on Mt. Moriah, you can see the most spectacular view of Jerusalem. It is our highest point in the city."

She was surprised that of all the nights they might go there, he would invite her this evening. Fresh in her mind was Bilhah's riveting account of the temple dedication, its effect upon her still lingering.

Noticing that the King had not yet let go of her hand, she wondered at how comfortable they had become together. He led her out of the palace, and she took a deep breath of the cool, crisp air.

"Isn't this a rare display of beauty?" spoke the King. He was enthusiastic to point out to her everything magical about this night in his beloved country.

As their eyes adjusted to the darkness, the stars came out of their hiding places. It seemed that the sky had practiced this pleasing performance just for them.

"So tell me," began the Queen, "how long did it take you to construct this sacred edifice?"

"For over seven years, the workers labored to perfect the design. I began the building after having been King for four years. You see, completing this dream, passed down to me from my father David, was the most important task assigned to me. He wanted to build the temple himself. It was he who had the plans from God for the structure. His passion to see a place for the Presence of his God was so great that he provided from his personal treasure—gold, silver, bronze, iron, wood, onyx, precious and marble stones in abundance."

"He must have been an amazingly generous man, obviously driven by a vision," commented the Queen.

"He was an extremely benevolent man. And I have never known a more passionate man in his love for God. He taught me the ways of Jehovah, admonishing me in his last days to cherish God and always seek Him first. He said that if I sought Jehovah, I would find Him, but if I forsook Him, He would cast me off."

The Queen had a hard time imagining Solomon forsaking his God. It saddened her to even entertain that possibility. This idyllic kingdom surely was meant to last forever.

"What a destiny you inherited!" spoke the Queen.

Continuing to converse, they came closer and closer to the thick wall surrounding the Temple. Already, the two escorts were slightly ahead opening up the gate doors as they approached. The Queen had never been this near the temple. Since her country did not believe in Jehovah, she had tried to maintain a respectful distance from this palace that was built for the Jewish God and not for the honor of man.

Solomon continued, "As you know, I was so young when I became King and felt like a child. My father told me to be strong and courageous, to fear not nor be dismayed, for God was with me and would never forsake me in this work. I suppose my father knew that I needed to hear those words.

"I completed the temple and established that the worship should be in accordance to the Davidic order established by my father. That is why as we approach, you may hear music and singing. Jehovah is worshiped day and night."

As the Queen drew closer and closer to the steps leading up to the temple, her heart began to beat faster and faster. The structure looked like a powerful and strong fortress crowned with Phoenician elegance overlooking Jerusalem.

Solomon commanded the torch bearers to assist the Queen up the stairs. She at last stood upon the temple porch and turned around to glimpse one of the most magnificent views she had ever seen. Soft hues of candlelight decorated the entire city as it glowed brilliantly in the night.

Solomon took his own torch to join the Queen while she peered upon his favorite view in all Jerusalem. Although the beauty before her was indescribable, in this moment, she shifted her eyes to behold the King as he made his ascent to the house of the Lord. It was as if time stopped and she saw within his soul. What she saw was a man who deeply loved his God. Even in the dimness of the night, a celestial brightness stayed upon him. The passion within the King shone forth through his face, his features. Her heart was racing. The evidence of divine love shining upon his countenance was gripping her innermost being.

Then what she had longed for happened. She felt the Presence of Jehovah. Words could not describe the loveliness of Him. She saw Him through the eyes of her heart for the first time, unlocking her ability to experience His great ocean of love for her. He was powerful, yet gentle; strong and kind at the same time. As He looked at her, she was flooded with pure joy. She felt everything within and without was transformed into a paradise of delight. Currents of Divine Life pulsated through her whole being. She wanted to commune with God endlessly. Perpetual peace and blissful contentment satiated her soul, and she never wanted to leave this ocean full of heavenly treasure. Then, she became breathless and was overcome by the exquisite revelation of it all.

The next thing she knew, she found herself lying against Timothy's breast with the King kneeling beside her, his hand upon hers. She slowly opened her eyes.

"How are you, how are you?" repeated the frightened King as he tightened his grip on her hand.

A smile of ecstasy spread across her face. For a long time, she did not speak. Then she began to exclaim to the King, "It was a true report I heard in my own land of your acts and sayings and wisdom."

Supposing that such a response meant she was not ill, Solomon hugged her with relief.

She continued, "I did not believe it until I came and my own eyes had seen. Behold, the half was not told me. You have added wisdom and goodness exceeding the fame I heard."

Then she realized that coming from behind the doors of the temple was a crescendo of the voices of worshipers echoing the truth that poured from her heart.

"Oh, give thanks to the Lord, for He is good, for His mercy and loving-kindness endure forever," came the sound of angelic melodies reverberating the words over and over.

The Queen continued speaking, "Happy are your men! Happy are your servants who stand continually before you hearing your wisdom."

Timothy was caught up in this moment that the Queen was experiencing. As he watched a transformation happening before his very eyes, an even more astonishing thing happened.

The Queen burst into jubilant exaltation to the God of the Jews. She began to bless Jehovah. An atmosphere of true adoration enveloped her, and she worshiped Him. "Blessed be the Lord your God. Because the Lord loved Israel forever, He made you King to execute justice and righteousness. I am so happy that I came to experience the fame of the person of Jehovah and the King He delighted to set on the throne of Israel. Many spectacular reports have spread throughout the earth about this kingdom. But the half has never been told!"

That night beneath the Jerusalem skies, the cluster of people upon the temple porch seemed small. But contrary to their humble appearance, the grandest of moments had occurred. This beautiful Queen had embraced the God of the Jews. Forsaking all other gods, she intended to love Him forever.

27

The rest of the evening was somewhat of a blur to the Queen. She vaguely remembered Timothy and Marion helping her into bed. For the entire night, she slept in the sweetness of the dramatic encounter. In her sleep, she ruminated on the divine revelations resting in her soul.

The next morning when she awakened, a sea of contentment and rich satisfaction like she had never experienced before flooded her being. She recalled her whispered prayer of longing to experience the God who had made Himself known to Bilhah and all who were present at the dedication of the temple.

Jehovah had answered her prayer in that breathless moment when she laid upon the temple porch and experienced the richest love that she had ever known. She had, no doubt, enjoyed the highest form of pure pleasure when she encountered Jehovah's love for her. The revelation of His loveliness empowered and impassioned her to love Him in return. She found unending delight as she beheld the beauty of His mesmerizing attributes.

Now she knew that He was the God she had always dreamed of having in her life, only He was far more wonderful than she ever imagined. Certainly, the treasure her heart had longed to find had been discovered, transporting her from the oppressions of false gods into the delights found from adoration of the true God. The passions of heaven seemed to pour into her.

How could she describe what had happened? Then she realized that she had been enraptured in a divine encounter of intimacy with the Living God. Yes, that was it. Intimacy was the perfect description. She had never known the bliss of being deeply and entirely loved by Someone so indescribably amazing. She could not put into words the glory of His perfect love. She wanted to love Him in return. She was humbled. She was empowered. Yes, she was speechless.

The Queen recalled a psalm that Solomon had read to her. It was written by his father, King David, speaking of the one thing that he asked of the Lord. When she first heard of it, she remembered imagining what she would ask of the Lord if she could have just one request. King David asked to dwell in God's presence all the days of his life and behold forever the beauty of the Lord.

In that moment, she understood for the first time King David's request. That must be why they called the king a God-gazer! She could not have imagined how powerful experiencing this beauty David spoke of would be. She thirsted for more and more exposure to Jehovah's delightful loveliness. She yearned to live in the place of perpetual revelation of His sweet attractiveness. Her hunger to know Jehovah more had been fueled by mere exposure to His sheer beauty.

The Queen had come to Jerusalem searching, but she now felt a call of destiny gripping her heart. She passionately desired to alter the course of her nation. No longer could her people be oppressed by following after the delusions of false gods. She must introduce Sheba to Jehovah. Then, they could become prosperous inwardly as they were outwardly. Now that she knew this God, the citizens of her country must know Him as well. She would return bringing with her the purest treasure of all.

Propping herself up in bed, she longed for Abigail. Her beloved friend had always been the main person she could confide in about personal matters. She wanted to share with her everything that had happened since leaving Sheba. Then she recalled waking up on the temple porch leaning against Timothy. Of course, this was her answer; she needed to talk to him because he had witnessed the unusual happenings the night before.

Calling for Marion, the Queen hurriedly began getting ready for the day.

"Marion, I wish to have my morning tea with Timothy."

"Yes, my lady," she replied.

"Oh, and, Marion, please arrange a private setting in the courtyard."

Marion bowed and quickly left to make the arrangements, leaving the Queen with the other attendants.

After the Queen's preparation for the day, Timothy arrived and was seated with her at the table. They were served fresh breads, jam, and tea while they enjoyed viewing some freshly cut flowers in a golden vase.

Timothy had never been alone with the Queen to dine. After the unusual happenings of the prior evening, he was beginning to feel a little uncomfortable.

"Welcome, Timothy," spoke the Queen.

"Thank you. I hope you are well this morning," he replied.

"Never have I been better," she answered, beaming as though she held a secret within.

"Timothy, I awoke this morning missing Abigail terribly. I have always confided in her. In her absence, it just seems right that I might discuss with you how it is that I have arrived at my conclusions about the God of the Jews. There are no secrets between us. Whatever you hear me say, you can and must share with Abigail upon our return."

"It is my pleasure," responded Timothy.

"I know that you witnessed a dramatic happening last night at the temple. I would love to tell you a little about my journey up to that moment."

"Of course, my lady."

"You see, Timothy, it was only slightly more than a year ago that I knew nothing about the Jewish God, Jehovah. When I began to hear the reports of Him, I felt a hunger stirring in my heart to know more. I became so thirsty for understanding that over time I was willing to risk my time, comforts, and even my reputation to begin the quest which led us to Jerusalem.

"I came to Solomon searching from a place of great need. Although outwardly a wealthy monarch, inwardly I was empty. I asked perplexing and difficult questions of him. Solomon answered all of them, ministering to my every need. With the passing of time, I was able to commune with him concerning everything that was on my heart. Eventually, my questions were quieted, and I became a devoted listener as well. Words of wisdom became like honey to me.

"I began to perceive things I could not see before. Just observing the servants of the palace or the cupbearers, I could discern the fullness of joy surrounding them. My revelations intensified until the moment that you witnessed on the temple porch. I had never truly lived until I worshiped Jehovah there for the first time.

"Timothy, Jehovah is my God, and beside Him, there are no others.

"Timothy," she said again, "you must know Him. We all must know Him. Our whole traveling family must know the wonders of His extravagant love. You see, our hearts truly have been made to be occupied by God."

The bravest man the Queen had ever known sat before her with tears in his eyes. The meek expression upon his face spoke volumes of his openness to hear and yes, receive this God, who had captivated both the Queen's heart and his.

It was then that the Queen heard cheers. She knew there had to be a spontaneous response to some sort of welcomed news.

Moments later, she heard someone approaching. "Please, come," she spoke.

Marion entered. "Your Majesty, a courier has arrived with news from Abigail."

"Please urge him to come quickly!" she said as she noticed that Timothy had already leapt to his feet.

The messenger arrived, appearing almost out of breath. He handed Timothy the sealed manuscript.

Timothy could hardly contain himself as he tore the letter open. Everyone braced themselves, eager for the news.

"I have a daughter. She looks like her mother!" he exclaimed.

The Queen clapped her hands with great joy. "Timothy, may I be the first to congratulate you." Forgetting herself, she stood to her feet and reached for his hand. Clasping it in hers, she could only think of Abigail and the gift of this news to Timothy. Robust laughter could be heard in the background. The Queen was dizzy with excitement. So much had happened. And the good news just kept coming!

While the celebration continued, not too far away in his palace, eating alone, sat King Solomon. He could not stop thinking about the scene he had witnessed on the temple porch. This monarch had captivated him. He related to her on so many levels as a true comrade, both sharing similar life experiences. The one major area of difference between them had now been eradicated.

Could it truly be that she had left her gods behind forever to embrace Jehovah? He had never witnessed a more beautiful miracle than what he saw as she lay breathless before the temple doors, with the sound of heavenly worship echoing from the temple. What a sight!

Throughout Jerusalem, rumors abounded. Everyone was curious about his relationship with the Queen of Sheba. He had spent much time with her since her arrival. They could be seen touring and conversing together throughout Jerusalem. Did he long to take her as his wife, they wondered. Did they love each other? Such speculations swirled about the city.

28

The Queen was on a mission and had scheduled a time to meet with everyone who had traveled with her to Jerusalem. She had high hopes for them that they would be the perfect messengers to carry back to Sheba the knowledge of Jehovah. Yet she was not sure how they would receive the news of her transformation. Perhaps they were already prepared to hear her story, for they also had been exposed to the witnesses surrounding them in this city. Surely, they had been watching her responses, eager to take their cues from her. Perhaps some of them had already been converted, but dared not say.

The Queen found them eager to hear her report. They seemed absolutely open to the God of the Jews. For since they arrived, they also had seen, heard, and experienced much to make their hearts tender and open for this moment. Embracing her revelation of Jehovah, they enthusiastically accepted the newly found sense of duty to be messengers of this good news, that is, except for Marion. The Queen could not understand her handmaiden no matter how hard she tried. Marion did not want to hear any more about the Israelite God. However, the important focus was that a nation was about to be transformed. The course they were traveling would be forever altered.

The Queen had arranged a meeting with the King. He was curious to hear what she had to say. This was the first time they had seen each other since the wondrous evening spent at the temple. They heartily greeted each other, and as soon as she was seated, the Queen began talking.

"It seems that our God has turned my life upside down, in the best kind of way," she pleasantly spoke. "Already I have become busy with the task of imparting the same glorious revelations I have received to my staff."

Solomon had come to admire her straightforward approach. This woman who was effortlessly emotive was also an assertive leader. She possessed a soft heart to receive deep revelations and also a brilliant mind.

She confidently continued, "Is it not true that there are scrolls filled with divinely inspired writings about Jehovah?" She did not stop for him to answer. "I know that your father David wrote many psalms and that you yourself have authored poems containing words of great wisdom.

"Could you provide copies for us of some of the manuscripts? We could study them here and also take them back with us to Sheba. My country must know the truth of Jehovah. We would also welcome Israelite teachers to instruct us in His ways."

Solomon could hardly believe what he heard. All his doubts subsided about the validity of her experience. She was now a woman with a mission. And she managed to get straight to the point.

"Whatever you ask of me, I will do for you," he replied. "From this day forward, as long as the citizens of Sheba remain in Jerusalem, I will send my wisest teachers for instruction in the ways of the Lord. Benjamin, one of my best, shall begin meeting with your staff immediately."

Now that she had received assurance that her requests would be granted, the two rulers enjoyed a relaxing visit. The King never ceased to be amazed at the endless issues addressed to him by the Queen. But somehow, he never tired of them.

29

The Queen could not quench her thirst for the readings from the Holy Scrolls. Each day, she and all the servants would gather and enjoy mornings of teaching from the writings about Jehovah. Often, after they were done, she would walk alone in the courtyard gardens and meditate on what she heard.

The time to return to Sheba was nearing, she felt. Even though departing from Solomon would be as difficult as leaving Abigail, perhaps she must leave before matters became more difficult. However, before she could deal with this, there was an important part of her journey to complete. She had to present the gifts to Solomon that she had brought from Sheba. This was the perfect time. For the giving of them was now much more than a ceremonial obligation. Rather, it was the culmination of a journey that had altered her life forever. She had given of her time to come to this country. She had given of her mind and eventually her heart. Now it was the time to give of her possessions. Moreover, with joy and overflowing gratitude, she would not only be giving the treasures of Sheba to Solomon, but to Jehovah as well. Not that He needed her wealth, but that she needed to give to Him.

Startled from her thoughts by Marion, she was given a message from the King. He requested that she come in the afternoon and stay for dinner at the palace. What a well-timed invitation! She could arrange for her gifts to be made ready for presentation to the King. With this thought, she became increasingly beside herself with excitement. She never realized that giving could be so exhilarating.

"Marion," she exclaimed, "get me Tamrin! We have important arrangements to make."

Marion left the room, and the Queen thought about how complicated her assistant seemed. Not even Benjamin, a skilled teacher of the sacred writings, had been able to break through her hard shell. His words of advice to the Queen were to be patient. Receiving the truth of God had to be a work of the heart and not forced, he said. Benjamin had decided to invest more of his time with Marion. It was obvious that she did not understand the changes taking place around her.

The Queen had begun to question how it was that Marion was picked in the first place to be her attendant. The awkward-ness felt between them was painfully clear. To complicate matters more, it had been Abigail's idea, and she had agreed to it.

The situation also made the Queen very aware of the chal-lenges that were ahead in Sheba. Only God could change a heart. It was then that she knelt in prayer and began to call out to Him for Marion and all those of Sheba who did not know Him.

The Queen and Tamrin spoke for what seemed like a long time. Marion held their meal until she was concerned they would not have time to eat it. When finally they came through the corridor, she ran ahead to alert the servants. Marion would not miss the coziness of their lavish apartment. She knew that her coworkers would be sad to leave behind the life they had known in Jerusalem, but for her, returning to Sheba would be a dream come true.

Sitting pensively in her room, the Queen could not stop thinking about the gifts they were about to give to Solomon. She had heard of the beautiful things he had made from gifts that he had received. From the almug wood that had been given to him, he had made steps for the house of the Lord and also harps and stringed instruments for singers. If this earthly King made beautiful things from the gifts he received, how much more beauty might Jehovah create from the gifts that were given to Him! Could it be that in giving Him her heart, He would make her a staircase for others to travel into His Presence or might he make her life into a living instrument of worship? In her heart, she could imagine Jehovah giving extravagantly to those who gave extravagantly to Him.

30

Timothy accompanied the Queen as she entered Solomon's palace. The King, at first, seemed surprised that Tamrin was with her as well. But the eagerness on their faces replaced any disappointment he might have felt with curiosity. Whatever they were keeping a secret must be interesting indeed.

"King Solomon," spoke the Queen. "I pray that you will accept our spontaneous plans as a pleasant surprise for your afternoon."

Once again, the King had no idea what to expect from this lively woman. "Continue," he replied. "What is contributing to your curious behavior?"

With the sincerity of an angel, she spoke from her heart. "When I decided to travel to Jerusalem, I was told that I would sacrifice much. I possibly would face unknown dangers—thieves, robbers, savage storms, in addition to the uncomfortable circumstances of the harsh desert travels. I could face the misunderstanding of the citizens of Sheba or the loss of life in perilous encounters. I would have to endure the monotony of endless miles of uneventful traveling. Many of these forewarned events did occur. As well, now we must soon embark through unknown territories on our return trip.

"What I have to say to you, dear King, is that the journey has been worth the price. I have discovered true treasure. I will never relinquish the sacred riches that have been given to me. The journey has been worth it! So worth it, so incredibly worth it!" With each declaration, her passion became more evident.

"As a token of our deep gratitude, I want to present to you some treasures of Sheba. They do pale, though, in comparison to what we have received from your kingdom."

Tamrin stepped forward and motioned to the servants to bring before the King the chests full of surprises. The Queen gave the king 120 talents of gold and great stores of costly and rare spices of Sheba. She gave him an abundance of precious stones as well. Never before and perhaps never again would such bountiful gifts be given to Solomon.

The King was humbled. This lavish act of gratitude left him momentarily speechless. When he did begin to talk again, he earnestly tried to thank them for their outpouring of generosity. Solomon was overwhelmed with motivation to give lavish gifts in return to the Queen. He insisted that there was no desire of hers that he would not grant. He gave her gifts from his personal royal treasury, besides insisting he give her all she wanted, whatever she asked.

The afternoon continued like a grand celebration. Solomon enjoyed the childlike joy that filled the room. The complexities of governing a nation were far from his mind. Like two youngsters, the King of Israel and Queen of Sheba laughed and enjoyed themselves into a state of royal ecstasy.

The time for dining drew near and Tamrin excused himself. The King was thrilled that he could have a meal alone with the Queen. They were ushered into an exquisite private dining area. Upon entering the room, he was pleased to hear his favorite music flowing from the musicians next door.

As the door closed, the Queen walked toward her chair, when she felt Solomon's hand upon her shoulder. How vulnerable she felt at his touch.

"Queen of Sheba, would you dance with me?" he asked.

After her shock subsided, a thousand yeses flooded her mind, but it took a moment to get one out in response. "Yes," she spoke with a nod.

The stately King drew her close, and for what seemed like a long beautiful dream, they effortlessly glided about the room like young innocents enjoying the delights of their first love. He slowly guided her in time with the music, and it was then the Queen realized that her head lay upon his shoulder. She had never known such feelings of safety that allowed to break forth her surrendering heart to this King. They danced in each other's arms for what seemed like a long time. She easily followed as he led her about the room. This was the first man she had ever felt she could, without hesitation, submit to his lead.

The music waned, and they stood in each other's embrace for a moment. She enjoyed the newly discovered feelings that came from observing his eyes as he looked at her adoringly.

"You are the most beautiful woman I have ever met," he spoke.

Her eyes met his, and as she melted beneath his gaze she leaned her forehead against him.

A knock at the door disrupted the blissful moment.

They were then seated at a beautiful table set for two. Aromas of the freshly prepared food filled the air. The Queen was hardly aware of what they were discussing, but she was acutely aware of what she was feeling.

After they ate for a while, the Queen began to share one of her deepest secrets. "Solomon, I mean, King Solomon," she said correcting herself. "Do you remember when you spoke to me of your dream at Gibeon when you were first King?"

"Of course," he replied.

She continued, "I told you that I also had a dream on the day that I became Queen."

"I remember," the King replied. "You seemed hesitant at the time to tell me more."

"From the day I was crowned until just before my decision to come here, I was tormented with nightmares. I was terrorized by them for all those years. My mother had them as well. She was dreadfully afraid of not pleasing the gods."

The King looked distressed as she spoke. But he was helpless to change the past, no matter how badly he wanted to protect her.

The Queen continued, "After I began to hear about Jehovah, one night I was having one of the dreadful dreams, when suddenly an invisible deliverer rescued me from the darkness and the cycle of terror has been broken ever since."

The King looked at her compassionately. It pained him to think of her in such darkness. At the same time, he was mesmerized by the power that brought such an abrupt halt to her nightly assaults.

"King Solomon, I have come to realize that Jehovah Himself rescued me. He was showing me His kindness even before I knew it was Him. He really is love, isn't He?"

The King could not contain his smile. The Queen glowed as she smiled back at him. Now she knew that there was nothing she could not share with the King. The night continued as one of the most perfect she had ever known.

31

The next morning, when the Queen awoke, she felt torn between two worlds. One world encompassed the increased awakening of her ardent love for the King, the other held the myriad of practical tasks that called to her. Until recent months, she had never allowed herself to entertain for any length of time what a devoted relationship with a man might be like. Now, she wanted to imagine a love like this in her life.

She let herself contemplate what kind of scenario might be suitable for a Queen. The stark realities settled upon her. She loved most everything about Solomon. Certainly, she had never known anyone whose wisdom she trusted more than his. She had never met a man who had loved and honored his God more than Solomon. What would life be like to be the wife of such a man? What would it be like to have a child by him? Would an off-spring of Solomon inherit the understanding heart so profusely displayed in the King? She was shocked to find herself having such thoughts.

He had certainly made her feel as if she were in a class of her own. But what did that mean? Besides, she could never leave her country for a man, whether he was a king or not. No, Sheba was her calling and she had best not even entertain such thoughts. The Queen jumped out of bed. She needed to arrange a meeting with Tamrin to begin discussing when they should leave Jerusalem.

Solomon had never admired a woman as much as the Queen of Sheba. She understood him in ways that no one else could. Her mind was brilliant. She magically brought out the child in him. Was there no way that they could maintain their friendship, their love? Did she have to return to Sheba? Could he convince her to stay? Deep down, he already knew the answer to his own questions. He longed for her ardently. Could he persuade her to marry him? Would she consider entering into a covenant relationship of holy matrimony and forever be his most treasured Queen? She was more special to him than any woman he had ever met. But would such a request be fair to her? If any love could last forever, he was confident it was theirs. He had known the companionship of other women, but how shallow and unsatisfying they were in comparison to what he had discovered in the Queen of Sheba! What they shared was unique. She would always be in his heart no matter where she lived. Surely, he could come up with an answer that would unite them forever in their love.

The Queen fought against the emotional tuggings of her heart toward the King. She wanted to deny them. Hastily, she set a date with Tamrin for their departure. She informed her Shebean companions of the day they would leave. The Queen sent messages to the palace, so that the King would not hear the news from someone else.

The announcement caught Solomon off-guard. He had hoped for more time to process the dilemma of his heart. He called for one of his larger Egyptian chariots to be brought. He had to speak with the Queen. When he arrived at her apartment, the whole staff was surprised at his unannounced visit. Quickly, the Queen was informed of his arrival, and she made her way downstairs where he awaited her.

"Would you do me the honor of coming with me for an outing?" he asked.

The Queen nodded and turned to Marion for assistance to gather what she would need to depart with the King. Solomon personally helped her into his chariot. In Sheba, she would have never traveled unaccompanied by a guard, but somehow, the invitation of a King seemed justification for an exception. He headed for the countryside of Jerusalem. She was thankful for all the noise created by the horse and chariot as it sped along the rugged road, so she could collect her thoughts before she spoke.

Solomon located his favorite spot to be when he was alone. The Queen felt unsettled. Never had the King arrived unannounced. The struggles of her heart were surfacing quicker than she could subdue them. She sat in silence as they came to a halt. There, in the quiet of the wooded area, the King began to bare his heart to her.

"I am a hostage held captive by my love for you. You are the fairest among women, like a lily among thorns in comparison, altogether beautiful. Your love is sweeter than wine to me. Would you remove my anguish caused by even the thought of being separated from you? I cannot let go of the newfound home my heart has found with yours. I want our love to last forever. Would you make my heart glad by becoming my bride?"

The Queen had no words to respond to his question. She was exploding inside with emotion. Her heart was beating so fast that she felt she could not breathe. Looking into his eyes, she saw him longing for her response.

Trembling with restrained emotion, she answered, "Your words are exceedingly pleasing to me. They comfort and delight my heart. I have not loved any man before you, only you are chief among all others. The whole of my heart loves you."

She began to cry uncontrollably. Leaning her head upon his shoulder, she could not stop the tears. The King dared not pressure her, but held her as though he would never let go. Slowly, her sobbing subsided, and they sat in total quiet.

At last, the Queen softly spoke again. "Might we go to the temple? I need to speak with our Jehovah."

When the Queen arrived back at her apartment, Solomon entered with her. He asked for Tamrin. They met together for a brief unscheduled meeting. The King told him of the banquet planned in honor of the Queen on the evening before their scheduled departure. He also discussed arrangements for the Queen to spend the night in the palace afterward, so that the last of the packing could be completed without inconveniencing her. Then the King left as abruptly as he had arrived.

That night, the King walked to and fro within his bedchamber. He was acutely aware that the Queen had not given him an answer. Never had he felt so lovesick. She had ravished his heart. Yet he knew, for wisdom's sake, he must leave her alone to process the course of her future. He found himself on his knees. Face uplifted, he looked up into the Jerusalem sky. Soaking in the comforts of Jehovah, he sought calm from the storm within.

Suddenly, he heard a knock at the door. The servant announced the arrival of his mother, Bathsheba. *How unusual*, thought the King.

"Please help her in," spoke the King.

Approaching the door of his bedchamber was a small bent-over woman, his beloved mother. He gently pushed the hood of her cloak back upon her shoulders. He kissed her and led her to the foot of his bed, helping her to sit.

"My Mother, my Mother, you have blessed me by your presence this night."

She hugged him and then held his face between her hands. "I cannot stop thinking of you this day," she spoke in a frail voice. "A mother always knows when her child needs prayer."

He looked into her tired yet wise face. She had a classic beauty, not yet diminished by the fine lines etched upon her face.

He could not hide his heart from her. "Mother, I have come to deeply love the Queen of Sheba. I want her always by my side."

They sat in silence for a moment.

She looked at him compassionately as she spoke, "I have heard from many sources that the two of you have become very close."

Solomon had tears in his eyes when he answered, "No other woman could ever compare with her."

She put her arms around him, saying, "I understand, my son, I understand."

Curious about what she had heard, he asked, "What are the people saying about my relationship with the Queen?"

"Most are intrigued. Some are confused. They do not quite understand the foreigners' claims to now be followers of our God," she answered.

"As you know, Mother, God has filled me with desire and vision for all people to know Him. You, yourself, heard my prayers at the dedication of the temple."

"Yes, yes, I remember," she answered.

"Mother, this is an answer to my prayer, for the visitors from Sheba to become followers of our God."

"And what of the Queen?" she asked.

"She was the first to openly believe," King Solomon said proudly.

"I am so happy," his mother replied. "My son, do not be troubled. I understand what it feels like to be entangled in the judgment of others. God knows your heart and has given you understanding of His intentions toward the nations. You are privileged. And as for your feelings for the Queen, God understands."

As Solomon's mother left the room, he looked up and thanked God for answering his prayer. He did not know exactly what it was that his mother said, but her visit left his heart in the peace he had longed to find.

32

Marion felt stretched thin these days. Her ability to focus on all the responsibilities pertaining to the Queen had become even more challenging. Increasingly, she was pulled in additional directions to make sure the packing for their trip home was completed on time. She knew that her position was one of high honor. However, early in the journey, she reluctantly resigned herself to the fact that she would never be "Abigail" to the Queen. Secretly, she was sick with longing to return home to Sheba. Packing was her only comfort because then she was reminded that their return was imminent.

"Abigail, Abigail," she heard from the sleepy Queen as she awoke.

Perplexed, Marion was not quite sure whether to respond or not. She knew the Queen would prefer that Abigail be with her, but the fact was, she was not. Trying to overlook the mistake, she entered the Queen's chamber.

"Yes, my lady."

"I need you to send a messenger to the King. Tell him it is important that we meet," spoke the Queen.

"Would you like your morning tea?" asked Marion.

"Yes, and then I will dress for the day as soon as possible."

Marion nodded and left in a hurry. She felt overwhelmed and frustrated that the Queen never even realized her mistake.

Even the Queen was surprised at how quickly they heard back from the King. While Marion was hurrying to complete the last details to prepare her for the day, they heard a knock at the door. Then, the servant spoke, "The King is requesting another outing with you in his chariot."

"Yes, of course," replied the Queen, "tell him I am coming."

When she entered the room where the King waited, she looked into his eyes. She felt that she never, ever wanted to look away from him. He took her hand and bid her come with him.

As they left Jerusalem, heading to the countryside, she reached and clutched his arm. Never saying a word, once again they arrived at his favorite spot. He turned toward her and searched her expression, hoping to find a clue for what her words might be. He hoped, he yearned, he waited.

"Last night," the Queen began. "I fell into a deep sleep. It seemed as though all the night I was searching for the one I loved. I was asleep, but my heart was awake. I searched all through the city, all through the streets, but I could not find him. My soul longed for him, but he was no place to be found. I called, but he did not answer. I was simply sick to be with my beloved. The more fervently I sought him, the more my love for him was awakened.

"And then, I found the one my soul loved. I held him and would not let go. You, King Solomon, are my beloved!" She became quiet briefly, but it seemed like hours to the King. "I would be honored to be your bride!"

He saw in her eyes what he had longed to know. Her sweet words affected him like he had just heard masterfully played instruments. They were as exquisite music to his ears.

At that moment, a dove landed on the tree limb just in front of them. Turning to her, he spoke, "You are my dove, my perfect one, now I know that you are mine, irrevocably mine," said the King.

"Yes," she replied, "I am yours, and you are mine." With unconcealed eagerness, she wanted to begin her life with him.

"Beloved," she said, "why do you call me your 'dove'?"

"You see, my love, God has made the eyes of a dove special. They can only focus on one thing at a time. I saw today that focus in your eyes for me, and I am undone.

"I have observed pairs of doves mated together for life. They watch each other. They sit together, they fly and alight together, synchronized to live as one always. You are my precious one, and I shall call you my dove."

She once again enjoyed the King's amazing skill for taking some unique attribute from one of God's creatures to depict a divine perspective. She was thrilled to be called his dove.

"But how should we proceed? My servants are all busy packing for our departure. I know that your staff is preparing for the banquet."

The King had an idea. "Let's have the banquet as planned. We shall complete our original plan and include the announcement of our betrothal. Let's expand the event to host a celebration for our new life together. It can be a surprise for everyone! Afterward, the priest can marry us in a private ceremony.

"The following day, we can travel throughout the streets of Jerusalem upon the bridal palanquin and greet all who want to share in our joy."

"But," she began, her mind spinning, "the banquet is only a few days away. I must tell Tamrin. I have to tell Marion, or she will suspect that something out of the ordinary is happening. After all, she will be the one to make sure I am a Queen prepared for her wedding."

33

When the Queen arrived back at her apartment, she summoned a meeting with Tamrin. Everything about her day felt unreal, from her dream, to her betrothal and now canceling their plans to leave Jerusalem. She had no time to reflect on how Tamrin might respond. She had to do what she had to do.

He arrived in the small library and was seated alone with the Queen.

"How are you, Tamrin, and the rest of the staff?" she asked.

"We are all extremely busy and a little apprehensive about the journey, but happily anticipating our return to Sheba."

The Queen thought to herself that perhaps this might not go as well as she had hoped after all. But she gathered her courage to continue.

"We have had a change of plans."

Tamrin did not seem the least bit concerned. He looked like he had anticipated some last-minute adjustments. She wondered how this hardy, adventurous man would react to her announcement. Hardly ever at a loss for words with her leaders, she felt awkwardness in not knowing how to proceed. So she simply spoke, "The King has asked me to marry him, and I have said yes."

Startled, he looked away, appearing to wonder if he heard her correctly. Then, looking down, he rubbed his nose as though it itched. At last, his eyes returned to her. Heartily, he spoke, "Wonderful! Splendid! Do you have any idea what new doors of opportunity this will open for our trade and commerce?"

Surprised yet amused by his response, she laughed. She could imagine him talking at length about all the new possibilities.

"Tamrin, you are perfect for your position."

"And, my lady, you are perfect for yours!"

"Tamrin, I love him very much."

He looked away, then down for a moment and scratched his nose. "Of course you do, my lady."

Somehow, Tamrin managed to make her laugh. She found his manner refreshing.

"Tamrin, we must keep this a secret until the King announces the news at the banquet. Only Marion must know."

"If it must be a secret, then a secret it will be, my lady. I only have one question. We will return to Sheba, will we not?"

"Of course, of course," she replied, finding it difficult to entertain that subject at the moment.

Standing up from her chair, she continued. "This has been a long day. Would you explain the situation to Marion for me? I will retire to my room and send her in to you. Also, adjust the schedules of the staff and relieve them from their packing. They will appreciate the relief."

"My pleasure, my lady," he responded as he stood and watched her exit the room.

Soon afterward, Marion entered. She was curious why Tamrin remained alone in the room after the Queen had already retired. *What did he want to say to her*, she wondered.

He spoke in his usual business-like tone. "Please be seated. The Queen has asked me to inform you of a change in her schedule. You will be the only staff person, besides me, to know this, and it must be kept a secret."

A sense of pride and superiority rose up in Marion upon hearing that she was the only staff who would know the secret.

Although the Queen could have told her personally, she thought to herself.

Tamrin continued, "The return to Sheba has been delayed, for the Queen and King Solomon are going to be married."

A blank stony stare peered back at Tamrin at this news. Marion was seething. Postponing the journey home was unthinkable.

Tamrin knew that something was not right. He could only think of one response at the moment.

"You know, Marion," he spoke, leaning forward in his chair, "you will likely be the only staff person privileged to move into King Solomon's palace with the Queen."

That had not occurred to her. She alone would have the honor. Perhaps she could adjust to the new circumstances after all. Skilled at covering up her feelings, she knew what she must do.

"I will prepare for the transition at once," she replied. "And since we are not to return to Sheba now, relieve me of some of my burden by assigning me help from other staff members." She spoke in a manner that felt more like a command than a request to Tamrin.

"Your wish is granted." he said.

Somehow, Tamrin felt he had resolved a crisis, but he was not quite sure what it was.

34

Timothy escorted Her Majesty and Tamrin into the palace celebration. As he accompanied them into the grand dining hall, he was thrilled at the reception given the Queen. Every single person stood and offered her their tribute. Music could be heard throughout the hall. Awaiting her in the center of the room was the King. He reached for her hand and gently guided her to the seat of honor beside him.

Timothy took his place stationed at one of the large entrances to the room. What a beautiful setting he beheld. The room was masterfully decorated with the Queen's favorite colors and flowers. The table settings were the most magnificent of any palace feast he had ever seen. And never had the Queen been more radiant.

There, the subjects dined and were entertained by lavish melodies and singers with extraordinary talent. The evening was perfect in every way. Eventually, the music came to a stop. Solomon stood before the people and summoned their attention.

"You all have been welcomed here to my palace home to honor this spectacular ruler from Sheba, who has blessed our city by her visit."

Turning to address the Queen, he continued, "In your honor, I present you, Queen of Sheba, with a copy of a prayer that my father, David, made for me before he died." He handed her a beautiful scroll that had her name etched upon it. "Our chief musicians have put to music the words of the prayer. It is my pleasure to honor you with my father David's words in song."

The most enchanting melody began to fill the room and heavenly voices blessed each listener with the words of the prayer of David for Solomon.

> Give the king Your judgments, O God,
> And Your righteousness to the king's Son.
> He will judge Your people with righteousness,
> And Your poor with justice.
> The mountains will bring peace to the people,
> And the little hills, by righteousness.
> He will bring justice to the poor of the people;
> He will save the children of the needy,
> And will break in pieces the oppressor.
> He shall have dominion also from sea to sea,
> and from the River to the ends of the earth.
> Those who dwell in the wilderness will bow before him;
> And his enemies will lick the dust.
> The kings of Tarshish and of the isles will bring presents;
> The kings of Sheba and Seba will offer gifts,
> Yes, all kings shall fall down before him;
> All nations shall serve him.
> And He shall live;
> And the gold of Sheba will be given to Him;
> Prayer also will be made for Him continually,
> And daily He shall be praised.[1]

The Queen could hardly contain herself as she heard the song. How could it be that King David actually spoke of Sheba before she had even heard the reports about Jerusalem? How could he have spoken about the gifts that would be given to Solomon? All of this was beyond her ability to comprehend. As the music waned, the Queen's eyes were filled with tears and she stood in wonder.

Solomon, still standing, spoke again. "Thank you, Monarch of Sheba, for fulfilling a part of my father David's prayer and prophecy for me, Solomon, King of the Jews."

Applause erupted as the whole room clapped in her honor. She stood to her feet and graciously waved in their direction. The Queen was honored that she had fulfilled David's prophetic utterances, bringing gifts from Sheba to both Solomon and his God. Thankfulness rose in her, and she also wanted to fulfill the next part of his prayer. "And let all kings bow down before him, all nations serve him." For she now was a monarch who bowed her knee to Jehovah and would do everything in her power for her nation to serve Him.

Timothy watched from afar. The musicians began to sing again the beautifully composed song. It was at that moment that he noticed a new visitor arriving at the palace. While the stranger was quietly received, he barely heard the whispering voice, addressing the priest and telling him that he would be taken to the guest area of the palace, which was beside the King's chamber. *How curious*, Timothy thought to himself. Why, that is most probably where the Queen is sleeping tonight. Puzzled, he comforted himself by the fact that the King must know the meaning.

Eventually, the applause ended. King Solomon and the Queen stood before the guests. At that moment, a musician sounded his trumpet and the rich spectacular notes filled the room. When the trumpeter finished, the room was quiet. The attention of everyone was on the King and Queen before them.

Solomon spoke again, "Jerusalem guests, thank you for honoring the Queen of Sheba. Now, would you join me in yet another reason to celebrate? I have asked the Queen to be my wife and she has said yes!"

A hush spread across the room. One by one, faces lit up by the charm of the news. A profound tenderness was felt by all. The King's words were soft and gentle as he looked upon his bride-to-be. An expression of awe was upon his face as he continued to address the people.

"The Queen of Sheba has come to my banqueting table. My banner over her is love. Tonight we shall be wed, and tomorrow we will tour the city upon the wedding palanquin. The finest wine shall now be served. Let the celebration continue."

The atmosphere was charged by the surprise of the announcement. Everyone made merry and enjoyed the gaiety of the moment.

Timothy, still stationed at the entrance way, was filled with pride at the news. He could not wait to tell Abigail that their beloved Queen was married to the most famous person on earth. *How deserving they were of each other*, he thought. The staff would be elated by the news. Now he understood why their departure had been delayed.

The palace guests continued to enjoy the wine and music. Long before the last citizens left the palace, King Solomon and the Queen slipped away to be wed in private. Marion waited in the guest chamber to prepare the Queen for her wedding night. She never imagined herself in this position. She received much satisfaction knowing she shared a moment in the Queen's life that Abigail could never know.

35

A warmth fell upon the Queen's face as the first rays of sun shone through the window of the King's chamber. She heard in the distance the singing of birds who also must have been enjoying the early morning sunshine. After relishing the softness of the rich bed cushions, she realized that the arms which held her throughout the night were gone. Pushing her long locks of hair to the side, she looked around the lushly adorned room. There sat the King at his table beside the window. He appeared to be in deep contemplation. She studied every detail of his silhouette, remembering the rich bath of embraces and kisses that they enjoyed throughout the night. Marital bliss was hers, and she hoped that she would never forget this canopy of love under which she basked.

"Beloved," she called.

As soon as he heard her voice, he arose and came to her side.

"Kiss me," she whispered in his ear.

The king was held captive by her words and by her beauty.

His kisses were like honey upon her lips as they enjoyed together the mysteries of marital splendor.

The hours passed, but time stood still for the Queen who was lost in the love of her King.

The King's only desire was to create for the Queen and for himself memories so rich that they would be forever upon their hearts, etched so deeply that not even distance or time could erase them. He wanted to fuel the burning of their love so that nothing could ever extinguish the flames of it.

Lying in the arms of her husband, the Queen spoke, "Whatever were you thinking about as you sat at your table this morning?"

He replied, "Most mornings I awake early. It is my habit to reflect on the ancient writings of Jehovah and spend time in prayer."

"And what were your reflections this morning?" she asked.

"I read again from the scrolls when Jehovah created man and woman and said it was not good for them to be alone. What enthralled me the most is that God put them in the Garden of Eden."

The Queen looked at her beloved questioningly. "And why would that interest you so?"

"Eden means delight," he answered. "It was God's idea that they start their lives together in a garden of delight. I was enthralled this morning by that thought."

The Queen had always been a thinker, probing beneath the surface, searching for the depth of meaning on any given subject. She must have met her match in Solomon. Excitement rose within her at the thought that as the cords of love drew them closer together, they could investigate the marvelous glories of God's intended messages.

36

King Solomon and his new bride had just returned from their bridal procession throughout the streets. The Queen had been touched by how excited the citizens seemed who greeted them. She wanted to remember every detail of those astonishing moments. Reflecting upon the beautiful palanquin which carried them, she recalled it was made from the cedars of Lebanon. The posts were silver, the back gold, and the seat purple. She would never forget the inside of the seat, which was covered with intricate needlework lovingly wrought by some of the women in Jerusalem. They were accompanied by stately, mighty men who surrounded them as they traversed the city. The people were genuinely warm and welcoming. She could see admiration in the eyes of the onlookers as they passed.

Now, back at the palace, Solomon took her by the hand. "Shall we have a private dinner?" he asked. "I have had to share you far too much on our first day married."

Blushing, she agreed, thinking she only wanted to be with him. She did not feel hungry at all.

"Beloved, I will meet you in our chamber. Have your meal, and I will wait for your return. Meanwhile, I will rest and freshen up for the evening."

Marion had been expecting her, waiting to draw a bath and anoint the Queen with fragrant oils and perfumed powders.

By the time Solomon returned, the Queen eagerly awaited him. The sound of his voice caused her heart to beat faster. "Your voice is sweet to me, and the whole of you brings me delight," she said.

"You are my garden of delight, make haste to come to me," he replied with his poetic words.

That night, each household in Jerusalem had its own story to tell. Within some dwellings, families were busy attending to small children. Some were taking care of elderly parents who lived with them. Others were cleaning up from a busy day, and some were preparing for the next. However, if the walls of the palace could talk, even then, it would be difficult to communicate the true joy and unending mirth found in the chamber of the King.

The next morning, the Queen was not awakened by the rising of the sun's rays. She awoke earlier to the flickering flames of the candle upon the table by the window. This time, she said nothing to her beloved. She just watched him. Face uplifted, his eyes were closed. Occasionally, he whispered prayerful words. She was immensely enjoying her observations. Sometimes, a peaceful smile would appear on his face, as though he had just heard some sweet secret and could not contain his gladness. This man had truly attained a close relationship with his God. She felt humbled that she had been given a seat on the front row to observe his private life. It was not until he reached for the scroll that he opened his eyes and saw she was awake.

"My dove," he spoke, "I did not want to awaken you."

"If I wake to behold you, beloved, I only awaken in joy," she said. "Come, hold me in your arms."

The King, leaning back against the headboard of the bed, held her as she leaned against his chest.

"What great truth are you meditating upon this morning?" she asked.

He was quiet as he stroked the locks of her hair. Pensive, he gazed upon her beautiful face. With his fingers, he touched her soft cheeks and outlined the curves of her lips.

"The richness of our love overwhelms me," he spoke. "It inspires me."

The Queen listened attentively.

He continued, "I cannot help but think that the passions of our bridal love are but a reflection of Jehovah's love for us. The richness of our union elevates me to seemingly new heights of revelation about Jehovah's desire toward us."

The King became quiet again and leaned his head back, closing his eyes. He was holding her as though she were a part of him. She rested there as his mind wandered into some sweet place of fresh revelation from above.

37

The next morning when the Queen awoke, it was still dark. She glanced across the room and saw the King as he sat by the flickering candle. This time, he was writing with the feathered quill pen, using the small well of ink beside the parchment. *This was different*, she thought to herself as she observed him. He appeared so deliberate as he wrote.

She felt inspired herself to pray and meditate on some of the sacred writings she had been reading. Not wanting to sit up and interrupt the King's focus, she lay still with her eyes closed, sensing the sweet presence of God in the room. She must have fallen back asleep, for the next time she opened her eyes, the room was flooded with sunlight and Solomon was quietly walking about the room. When he saw that she was awake, he looked elated. He pulled his chair to the bedside and took her hand in his.

"My dove," he began. "There have been times in the past when Jehovah would draw close to me and inspire me with words of truth to such a degree of intensity that I knew I had to write them on paper. The wise sayings and proverbs came to me that way. They are not my words, but the words of heavenly utterances put on paper." He paused and looked upward. "This morning, I began to experience that kind of visitation!"

She tightened her grip of his hand and asked with much curiosity, "What are you inspired to write about?"

"I have been a student of the love of God, but Jehovah seems to be giving me fresh understanding. I am falling beneath the spell of fresh discoveries, even as I dwell in the cocoon of my love for you. In this rich context of our bridal love, I sense a door of revelation springing open. I am grasping hold of deeper understanding. Jehovah Himself loves us as a bridegroom loves his bride. People may think me mad, but I am compelled to write about this lavish love. I must write the truths on paper. I want to know how Jehovah would have me depict this part of His heart. God's people cannot go about their lives unaware. They must know."

Oh, how the Queen loved him. She related to his passionate spirit. She could feel his drive and sense of mission. But she could not relate to the idea of crafting words on paper to reveal inspired utterances. She was quiet as she tried to digest this new concept.

Interrupted by a knock, the King answered through the door. The messenger relayed that one of his trusted advisers was seeking a few moments with him in the afternoon. Solomon consented.

The King spoke, "Sometimes, I find it difficult to return to ordinary affairs when Jehovah draws near. Yet I know that He is with us in all aspects of our lives."

That afternoon, Solomon greeted his adviser. "What brings you to the palace this fine day?" asked the King after they were seated together.

"As you know, my King, there are many issues to be addressed in governing the nation. Some are questioning your wisdom in marrying a foreign woman who serves false gods."

The King was infuriated by what he heard. "She may be foreign, but she does not serve false gods, she is now a follower of Jehovah."

"Do not take offense, my lord. I only want you to be aware of the rumors, for she is not a Jew. Perhaps the talk will diminish once you resume your governing activities."

"That will certainly not be soon. Not only do I have a new bride, I have been inspired by Jehovah to write. I am certain that I please Him by putting on paper the words given to me."

The adviser abruptly stopped talking. He knew well the anointing upon the King's prior sacred writings. He would not question the King's statement.

Continuing, the King spoke, "I may all but disappear for a time from the massive maze of governing activities. There is a season for everything. I might also remind you that the Queen and I have not even completed our week of banqueting and wedding festivities."

"I understand you well, my lord," answered the adviser as he bowed and dismissed himself.

The King decided to step outside for fresh air. The day was unusually hot and the wind very gusty. It was rare for Jerusalem to have a dust storm, but the King recognized the ominous look of the strange clouds in the distance. Jerusalem had not encountered such a storm in several years.

"We will stay inside tonight," the King spoke when he met up with the Queen. The howling winds could be heard in the background. "I need to warn the staff of a possible storm. Will you let Marion know?"

"Marion is not here. She is attending the required meeting at the apartment to study the sacred writings with Benjamin," replied the Queen.

"Very well," spoke the King. "I'm sure that Benjamin will take good care of her."

That evening, the Queen perceived the King's frustration after he had spoken with his adviser. She, knowing well the difficulties of ruling a nation, said nothing, as he fell into a deep slumber.

However, the Queen could not sleep as the winds raged outside her window. *At least she was not in a tent*, she thought, succumbing to a sick feeling as she remembered the desert storm that almost took her life. She could not stop the restless thoughts. The face of Marion, the bull's face of Ilmaqah, and the taunting words of Uncle Hanam kept coming to her. *How strange*, she thought, finally getting on her knees to pray. She knew for certain that her God was her protector, and she would no longer bow to fear.

The storm continued. Aware that Marion had never returned to the palace, she prayed for her safety. As uncomfortable as their relationship had been, she wished Marion no harm. Eventually, as the storm began to calm down, so did the Queen's spirit. An unusual peace settled upon her. She returned to bed and fell asleep beside the King.

The next day, Jerusalem was covered with a blanket of sand and seemed quiet compared to the roaring winds the night before. When a knock was heard at the palace doors, Benjamin asked to speak with the Queen. She was startled by his disheveled state. Covered in dust and sweat, he had nonetheless been insistent to speak with her.

"Benjamin, have you suffered any injuries?" she asked.

"My lady, I am only weary from a tempestuous night. You see, the storm approached as I was teaching about Jehovah with your staff. Marion, I fear, saw it as an opportunity to leave early before the full fury of it was upon us.

"She has always appeared unhappy to be at the meetings, as you know. Before I could stop her, she slipped out, mumbling something about getting back to the palace."

"But she never came back," said the Queen with great alarm in her voice.

"I know, I know, my lady. This morning, she returned to us at the apartment where we had all spent the night. Then she relayed to us what had happened. On her way back to the palace, she became caught in the fierce winds and had to quickly take refuge in an abandoned dwelling on the side of the road. The structure was so old and damaged, she was certain she would die. In her terror, she called on Jehovah to save her life, and she endured with only bruises from falling debris.

"After the storm subsided, she returned to the apartment and," he paused to gain his composure, "she is a different woman. She has come to know our God," he spoke with tears in his eyes.

The Queen was speechless. After she had a moment to process the report, she grasped Benjamin's hands in a display of gratitude. "God has truly answered our prayers," she said.

The King joined them and was soon rejoicing as well. He delighted in all that he heard. God was moving in wondrous ways.

Benjamin was leaving the palace when yet another man approached the entrance. He was dressed in the garments of Sheba, obviously a sailor. The Queen saw him through the open door and quickened her steps to meet him.

"Your Majesty," he spoke bowing before her. "I arrived by ship and have traveled for days to bring you an official message. The storm delayed me, but now I personally deliver to you a letter from Ashor."

She quickly reached for the parcel as the King watched beside her. She opened the letter, scanning the words. Suddenly, the King reached for her arm as color began to leave her cheeks. After he helped her to sit, she cupped her face in her hands and said not a word.

"What is it, my love?" asked the King.

After a long delay, the Queen responded, "We endured the night of the storm within the safety of the palace walls and have awakened to a new day. Marion begins her life anew, and Uncle Hanam has died." The Queen was still trying to process how curious it was that the news of both happenings came to her at the same time. A mixture of joy and sadness filled her being, but a mantle of peace rested upon her.

38

The Queen awoke earlier than usual and saw that the King was up as well. The candle lighting the room revealed him writing and writing and writing…

She waited for some time before speaking. At last, she asked, "How long have you been up, beloved?"

"I'm sure I do not know. When I awoke, I was seized by inspiration and excitement to write, so I did. The force driving me was such that I had to put the words on paper. What I am writing must be very important to Jehovah. The brilliant words of love flow effortlessly upon the pages and surprise me, as if I am reading them for the first time.

"Words can seem inadequate to convey the true depth of God's love. But today, I knew what I must do. I am writing a song, but not just any song, this will be the most excellent of them all. I am undone by what I see when I am caught up in the story, the song of love for those who seek the mysteries thereof to enjoy."

The Queen processed his words. She wondered if she was the sole witness of the birth of a sacred writing.

"Please read to me the inspired words," she requested.

The King pulled his chair beside her and by the flickering candle read to her. Never could she have anticipated the richness of the words. She had come to understand the God who ardently loved her, but this revelation that flowed from the pen of the King, she could have never guessed even existed. Deeper and deeper she went as she listened, into the depths of discovery of divine love.

Flowing upon the pages came the message the King hoped would reveal the immeasurable love of God for all who dared to open their hearts. He pondered the lives of his people and fervently desired to craft a story so captivating that all might come under the influence of the truths within the pages as he had. He wished to preserve the words forever in order to deliver the inspired message to all who read it.

Solomon rose early every morning to write the lyrics of love that he now understood in greater dimensions. More than ever, he awoke anticipating the discovery of more of this newfound treasure trove within and craft on paper the beauty thereof. He flourished in this atmosphere as he also enjoyed his life with the Queen. He wished he could choose to live forever on such a pinnacle of sacred pleasure, an open heaven of clarity, to behold the delights and love of eternity.

One of the greatest joys shared by the King and Queen was when he read to her by the light of the candle as the flame cast illuminations that danced about the room. Each morning, he would share what he had written. She listened to the poetic words and basked in the splendor of them. They easily found their way into her heart.

The Queen was the perfect audience for the King. She had always digested every word she could of his wise sayings and proverbs. Now, these truths were like exquisite rare dainties, and she savored every bite. The revelations of the King overflowed upon her. When she listened to the readings, she heard the phrases and personality of her beloved coming out in the words of the story. They would discuss what he wrote and talk endlessly of the mysteries found in the song of the love shared between the bridegroom and the bride in his story.

Days turned to weeks, and their routine never altered. The Queen was humbled that she had been blessed to be with the King during this unique season. How long would these days of heaven upon the earth last? She did not know. The road ahead held many unknowns for her. But with all her might, she knew she must give herself completely to these divine moments, so that at least the memory of them would never leave her. Deep inside, there would always be an understanding of how life could be lived. And even if she never had another season like this one, she had caught a glimpse of eternity.

39

One morning as the Queen awoke, she looked across the room and saw the silhouette of the King standing at the window looking over Jerusalem.

"Beloved," she called.

He crossed the room toward her and sat on the side of the bed.

The King spoke, "I have something to tell you. I am done with the writing. I have completed the words of the Song."

Elated, she answered, "You have finished a wonderful work, masterfully conveying the highest love of all."

Solomon, appreciating her affirming words, continued speaking, "I pray that it will be the greatest love song ever written. There will be those who read the words, drawing forth wisdom for marriage, and that is well and good. Others may read, simply enjoying it as a story, an allegory of love between a bridegroom and his bride. Some may think I have written a story of my own life. But best of all, there will be some who grasp the noblest of truth and catch a glimpse of God's passionate bridal love for them. They can draw from every angle of truth in the revelations of the song. May these individuals be transformed by the power of the knowledge that Jehovah is their bridegroom and loves them as His bride. Many waters cannot quench such love."

The Queen felt the warm embers of affection in her heart for the King. What intimate moments they had shared! In their brief time together, they had exchanged more rich experiences than most people would know in a lifetime. She reached for him and kissed him on his forehead, then on his lips.

"Let's go for one of our outings this afternoon to your favorite place," she said.

"Of course, of course, my dove, I will arrange for the chariot."

It was a beautiful day in Jerusalem when they arrived beneath the trees in their secluded place. The King placed his arm around the Queen, and she snuggled against him.

Teasingly, the King said, "I am thankful that there is no drama behind our drive here today as in the other times we have been here together."

The Queen laughed at his remark.

"Would you like there to be?" she teased.

"Only if the drama had a good outcome," he mused.

After a few minutes of quiet, the Queen said, "There is something I wish to share with you."

He looked at her, trying to discern the meaning behind her remark.

"I had a dream last night," she said.

The King remembered the last time they sat in that very spot. The Queen had begun their conversation then the same way. The outcome had been that she said yes to becoming his wife. He hoped to be so blessed by this dream.

The Queen continued, "The way my dream began last night was not unlike the last. I was searching frantically for the one I love. At least now I know who he is!"

"I am grateful to be reassured," he said a bit mischievously, still trying to be lighthearted.

Continuing, she said, "It seemed as though I searched all night for you—all through the city, all through the streets, but I could not find you."

He drew her close and became more somber.

"My soul longed for you. I called, but you did not answer. I called for you again. Then, out of the quiet night came the voice of a child. I turned around and there stood a youngster. He called out, 'Mother,' to me and I answered, 'Menelek!' In the youth of his being, I saw upon him the spirit of a champion. The spirit within you was also in him."

The King had tears in his eyes, and the Queen wiped her wet face as they embraced each other.

"I was comforted by having him at my side," she spoke, concluding her dream.

Flooded with emotion, the King wanted to ask if he had been in the dream. But he dared not. His heart was not yet ready to accept the inevitable.

They sat together and watched the sun until it began to set. Then they headed back to the palace, hoping to return before dark.

The chariot pulled up in front of the palace doors. The King walked around to assist the Queen from her seat. She stood, and he took her hand. As she maneuvered her foot forward, it caught on the edge of the chariot and she tumbled forward. The King caught her before she could fly onto the ground and held her in his arms. She saw the alarmed look on his face. He stood frozen and holding on to her as though his life depended on it.

She waited. Then, looking at him, she said, "You can let go of me now."

Her words hit him like the weight of stones thrown against his heart.

He looked at her and said, "What did you say?"

"I said, 'You can let go of me now.'"

Quickly, he placed her on the ground. Unharmed, she took his hand and walked toward the palace.

He was deeply troubled by her words. It was as though a coded message had come to him, telling him that now he must let go of her, but not only so that she would again stand on the ground.

Within the words was a still small voice saying that he had to let go for whatever her future held, wherever her destiny led her. The encrypted message stayed in his mind for days. He could not stop thinking about it. The words she spoke haunted him, although he realized that she never even knew what had happened. The message became so established within him that he knew Jehovah had spoken to him through the words of the Queen.

The force of the message did not interfere with the cherished moments they shared together. The King knew he could live with her forever and never grow tired of adoring her. He also knew that a factor that contributed to the depth of their relationship was that they shared similar experiences—the call to lead their nations being one of them. The Queen had said in the dream that she found comfort in their son when she could not find her beloved. He felt increasingly vulnerable. How could he know comfort in her absence?

40

The joy of their days together continued. It was a bright sunny day in Jerusalem. The Queen was just returning from the markets on the bustling streets of the city. She found the outings in the beautiful Egyptian chariot invigorating. Today, she had enjoyed the time alone to think during the drive there and back. The servants assisted her into the palace as she carried a parcel beneath her arm.

Immediately, the King greeted her. "I have missed you, although I find it marvelous when you enjoy your outings in this city that I love."

She kissed him on his cheek. "Today is so beautiful," she said. "Could I convince you to have dinner with me in the courtyard so that we can enjoy the night sky and all of its charm?"

"My dove, I think you could convince me of most anything!" he said as he smiled and looked forward to an evening outside in the fresh air.

Marion helped her prepare for the evening. In the past, their relationship had always been business-like. Seemingly overnight, the Queen's relationship with her had changed. They prayed together and discussed the bright future ahead for Sheba.

"Marion," the Queen spoke, "I do not think I have ever witnessed a transformation such as the one that has taken place in you. Your countenance, your attitude, why, your understanding heart is remarkable. I am thoroughly enjoying our kindred spirit and ability to talk so openly together."

The Queen continued, "I remember hearing the King speak of how God works all things together for good. Now I understand this truth in a new way."

Marion responded cheerfully, "I have never experienced a relationship transform so quickly! Just a short time ago, I thought I hated Abigail because I could never be like her for you. But now I know that I have my own unique place in your life, and I do not have to compare myself to her.

"After all, we have shared a lot together, and this history I can now treasure. I was with you when you almost died, when you fell in love, and when you first came to cherish Jehovah. These are no small happenings. And even if they were, it would not matter."

The Queen smiled. "I have to confess, there were times I wondered if we made the right choice when we asked you to travel here. But now, I have never been more sure that it was the best decision. Not only have you become my dear friend, but one day, when we return to Sheba, we shall be partners in our destiny. You will be a key person in the mission ahead. The job will be challenging, but we will be a strength to one another through it all."

Hand-in-hand, the King and Queen entered and were seated in the courtyard. They enjoyed each course of the palace food and laughed together as they discussed mundane matters, but mainly, they just enjoyed being together. They had watched the sunset and listened to the singing of the birds until at last the quiet came with the night.

The Queen was astonishingly beautiful in the moonlight, thought the King as he looked at her.

"Beloved," began the Queen. "With each passing day, I am more certain that I am with child."

She was so forthright and matter-of-fact, that he almost did not really hear what she was saying. So he replayed the words in his mind. She was with child! That meant she carried his seed within her!

"My love, this is an announcement that should have been heralded by trumpet! So it is true? You carry our child?"

"I am confident."

Heartily reaching to embrace her with rejoicing, he managed to knock over a water goblet, the noise of the crash interrupting the special moment.

So the King took her hand instead and sat back down. "I suppose I have heralded the announcement by creating my own grand noise!" spoke the King as he processed the news.

The Queen had already thoroughly considered every possible scenario that could be entertained by this development. The wonder of this gift had progressed into scrutinizing the realities of the course set before her. So at this point, her perspective was somber and pragmatic. But she did not want to quench the King's enthusiastic response and thrill with her announcement.

The King overflowed with ideas. "We will have to prepare for his birth. We will train him in all the ways of Jehovah! We will teach him how to govern a nation."

The Queen was silent.

The King became quiet. He harnessed his idyllic dreams.

They sat tightly gripping hands.

The King looked up into the Jerusalem skies. He could not escape the realities that he reluctantly faced. Before him sat the love of his life. He desperately tried to think of ways to persuade her to make Jerusalem her home.

"My dove, would you not consider staying with me forever?" he asked.

Her voice cracked as she spoke. "For a few glorious moments, I considered." Shaking her head, she continued, "I know that it would not be right."

He remembered her dream. He remembered the encrypted message that he had buried inside himself.

The Queen continued, "I believe it is safest for the baby if I travel as soon as possible. I have a brief door of opportunity to arrive back in Sheba before the birth. I have come to the conclusion that it will be safer for the infant to travel within me than to make the harsh journey after it is born. If I wait, I will be another year away from Sheba, my home, my country."

"But what about your safety?" the King sincerely questioned. "If you must return, I will send with you my most learned in the use of natural medicinal substances, the best physicians of Jerusalem. I will send with you our most experienced midwives. I am consumed with concern for your safety and the health of the baby."

"Yes, that would be good," acknowledged the Queen.

They both had to accept the difficult task of doing what was right, even when everything in them wanted to escape it. The numbness they felt because of this reality caused them to quietly call out to Jehovah for peace to carry through with the plans they knew were best.

The King did not know how much longer he had to enjoy such evenings with the Queen. He did not want the heaviness that encroached upon them since they began speaking about the Queen's return to ruin the wondrous news that she was with child. He wanted to hear her laughter again. "Then I shall return with you to Sheba," he spoke, hoping to solicit a response from her.

"So you shall hide in my trunk until we are on the other side of Moab, will you?" the Queen teased.

"Yes, and I will come out at night, and no one will ever know."

They laughed together. He had accomplished his goal. Perhaps if they could laugh together, they would not yet have to think about the inevitable.

41

The last day of the Queen's stay in Jerusalem arrived much sooner than it seemed it should. All the Shebean servants banded together to complete the packing. Solomon continually sent them supplies, food, and resources that might be needed on the long journey to Sheba. He was sending with them men who could teach the ways of Jehovah from the copies of the sacred writings they would take. Physicians and midwives would accompany them as well. Whatever Solomon thought would add to their comfort and safety, he gave.

The night that the King and Queen had not even been able to acknowledge was now upon them. It was their last night together. There would be no banquet. There would be no grand occasion to mark the end of the Queen's stay in Jerusalem. The King had arranged a meal for them in the private dining room of the palace—just the two of them.

They sat at the small elegantly set table. Gazing at each other through the soft hues of the lit candles, they talked and ate, but mainly, they shared their thoughts one last time. The musicians in the next room provided them with heavenly melodies, which descended like a healing balm upon their hearts.

The Queen was held captive by the King just as she had been the first time they ate in the room. She reached for the parcel that she had brought with her to the dinner. Placing the contents before the King, she watched for his response. There lay a beautifully woven tapestry, a coverlet for his bed. Within the crafted hues of purple thread was the silhouette of the Queen. The artist had crafted a magnificent work of art. The resemblance of the lady woven within the tapestry to the Queen was remarkable.

"Beloved, I wanted to give you a gift that might remind you of my love for you. As you read and pray by the flame of the candle, warm yourself with the cover spread upon your lap. At night, if you are cold, tuck it around your frame, that the warmth of it might remind you of the closeness of my heart. I had the Jerusalem woman weave strands of my hair into the fibers of the tapestry, so that a part of me would always be with you."

The King took the coverlet in his hands and pressed it against his face. "My dove, I am truly speechless."

The melody composed in the Queen's honor began to play. The King looked at her and tried to frame the moment in his heart. "I have arranged for the bridal palanquin to go back with you to Sheba, so that every time you ride upon it, you will think of me."

The Queen's thoughts returned to that day when they first rode through the streets of Jerusalem as husband and wife. She remembered every detail of its exquisite craftsmanship. She recalled all the mornings that the King read the inspired writings to her by the candlelight. Memory upon memory passed through her mind.

She began to speak as she savored each minute with her beloved. "You have given me so many precious gifts. I shall remember you always. You have given me your love. You have instructed me in the ways of Jehovah. And now you have given me a child, an heir to my throne."

"And you, dove, you are the Queen who will be a wonderful mother to our child. I know that you will raise him in the ways of Jehovah. For that, I am forever grateful." He reflected upon the moment he first met her. He thought about her as she lay breathless upon the temple porch. There would never be another woman like her—ever. In his mind, they were perfect together in every way.

He reached for a box upon the table. Opening it, he tilted it forward so the Queen could see the golden ring within it. "Take this with you, my dove, and give it to our child. It belonged to my father, David. Hopefully, one day, our son will come to Jerusalem, and I will know that it is him by the ring upon his finger."

"Of course, of course," she said. "He will be a wise king one day like his father. And yes, I will raise him in the ways of Jehovah."

The Queen remembered her dream. The young lad remarkably resembled his father. However, she then recalled that she never found her beloved in the dream. She did not know if she would ever see the King again.

Beneath the box which held the ring, the Queen noticed an ornate leather pouch. At the same time, the King reached for it. "I want you to take this with you as well," he said. Unveiling the contents, she saw a golden framework, holding the scroll of the song the King had written. Etched upon the gold at the top of the parchment were the words "Song of Solomon." The Queen took the scroll and held it against her heart. She closed her eyes and remembered the first time he began reading the words to her.

The King stood. "Will you allow me to dance with you one last time, my dove?"

She abandoned herself to his arms and followed his lead. She felt as if she were in the most brilliantly orchestrated moment that could be known between two people, and she never wanted it to end. *Was she in a dream or just the recipient of this gift of love,* she wondered. She traversed the room in his embrace. Peering into each other's eyes, they exchanged glances communicating the rich treasure they had found in one other.

Such torrents of emotion welled up within each of them until at last the King began to weep. Although he could barely speak, he managed to say, "My dove, let's go to Jehovah together." They knelt in the middle of the room, a King and Queen on their knees before the only One who could comfort them. There they lingered until they could bear to face the path unfolding before them. Only God understood the depth of their love. Only He could fill the void they would know in their separation.

High on the hill overlooking the city, within the solitude of his chamber, King Solomon stood at his window. With tears streaming down his face, he held the tapestry and watched in silence as the caravan disappeared in the far distance.

The months had passed too quickly. The Queen recalled the familiar sounds of the vast caravan that had been her home as they journeyed to Jerusalem. This time, the caravan would take her back to her dear Sheba. She left a different woman.

Tucked within the draped palanquin, she heard the city wildly celebrate her with cheers as she passed. She felt overwhelmed by her escalating emotions. Could she really be leaving? Everything felt unreal once again. In her hand, she clutched a small box, which held the ring that would be worn by her child. She had received the love of a husband and the gift of a child while in Jerusalem. Yet the dearest treasure she had received was one that she yearned to share with every citizen of Sheba. She would tell them of the great love of a God she had come to know, Jehovah, the only true God.

Epilogue

Over Thirty Years Later

Tucked in the midst of the city of Axum, a thriving trade post for Sheba, rose the exquisite palace that had become home to the royal family.

"This has to be the most beautiful day we have had since moving here," spoke the Queen as she looked toward the lavish gardens.

Menelek adored his mother and was thankful she still enjoyed good health. Sitting beside her, he was filled with gratitude. Everything he knew about God and ruling a nation, he had learned from her.

"Mamma," he spoke. "I have never seen you happier, you are the picture of contentment."

"Yes," she replied. "My life is richer and more fulfilling than I ever imagined it could be."

She turned toward Menelek, who looked like his father. "I am so proud of you. You wear wisdom as a crown, and you have been a delight to me since the day you were born."

"Mamma, how you continue to spoil me with your words, even after you have made me King."

"I shall never grow tired of spoiling you!" she answered playfully.

Menelek continued, "It is clear that heaven smiled upon your decision to move our capital across the Red Sea to this new location. Your desire to establish a city founded on the principles of Jehovah has brought immeasurable blessing. Peace, joy, and righteousness have met together here."

"God has been indescribably kind," she replied. "Through all the trials and triumphs, He has fulfilled His amazing plans. His faithfulness to Sheba is evident for all to see."

Suddenly, out of the garden, running toward her came her bundle of joy.

"Grandmamma," spoke the young lad. "Come with me! I have something to show you."

Gladly, she stood and offered him her hand. "Duty calls," she said gleefully to Menelek as she was led by her grandchild along the garden path.

"Look, Grandmamma! Look at the ants I found. They are working so hard, even though no one makes them. They must have stored up lots of food!"

She laughed at his words, even as she saw the reflection of Solomon in his astute observations.

The lad watched her as she laughed. "You are the happiest person I know," he spoke. "Please tell me your secret."

"Come," she said, "sit with me on the garden bench."

They sat together and she began to answer.

"Watch," she said, pointing to a passing butterfly. "If you seek God and his wisdom, no matter what difficulty tries to wrap around you, you will break out of any confining cocoon and be free like that butterfly! You will be joyful like me."

The Queen's grandson was beaming when he heard her words. She sat and watched him while he followed the butterfly down the path.

Fresh breezes filled the room as Abigail helped the Queen prepare for bed.

"Abigail, you have been a constant joy to me all these years. And now, at sixty years old, I still have you by my side. Look at us. We have aged, yet our spirits have never been stronger. We raised our children together, and now they make sure we have all that we need."

Abigail fondly touched the necklace she wore that the Queen had given to her many years before. "My lady, I shall wear this to my grave, forever as a token of our enduring friendship."

Reflecting, the Queen spoke, "I remember well the day I gave it to you. The night before, I had the redemptive dream which began to transform my life forever."

Abigail lit up. "How we have been changed by His love!" Helping the Queen into bed, she asked, "What shall I read to you tonight?"

The Queen's forehead wrinkled as she raised her eyebrows. "Please read to me the Song of Solomon," she replied as she reached for the ornate leather pouch beside her bed.

"I know that King Solomon's heart was not perfect toward Jehovah in his old age. The saddest season of my life was when I began to hear the news that his foreign wives had turned his heart from God."

The Queen removed the parchment and affectionately stroked the scroll with her hand as she continued to talk. "These words that you are about to read me will live forever. My beloved Solomon has been in heaven for over fifteen years. I am sure that all the good God put within him during his life-time lives on."

"Yes, my lady. As well I believe there will be a tender reunion when you meet him again in eternity."

Abigail looked at the Queen. She saw a woman who had no regrets, but only reflected the radiance that a grateful heart could give. She began to read the words of the sacred song to her, continuing until she noticed that the Queen had fallen asleep with a smile upon her face. It was then she realized that the small box holding the ring Solomon had given Menelek was held in Her Majesty's hand.

"Mother," came a whisper from Abigail's daughter at the door. "Come. You have gotten the Queen in bed, now let me help you. Father is waiting." Abigail quietly left, closing the door behind her.

The evening was magnificent. Menelek sat in the courtyard peering at the full moon with his son upon his lap. Rays of the moonlight warmly embraced them and illuminated the night.

"Look, Pappa! There is the most beautiful butterfly I have ever seen. It flies into the heavens.

"Grandmamma told me if I search for wisdom as a treasure, I shall be free like the butterfly. And my Grandmamma is a Queen!" he spoke proudly.

Menelek looked up at the sky. He was pensive as tears came to his eyes. "My son, let me see your face." The youngster looked into his father's eyes. "Always remember her words to you. She speaks the truth."

Jesus spoke these words as he addressed a crowd, whose eyes actually beheld the Son of God and whose ears heard firsthand the words of His mouth, yet, because of the hardness of their hearts, they could not perceive that the Savior of the world was before them.

> The queen of the South will rise up in the judgment with the men of this generation and condemn them, for she came from the ends of the earth to hear the wisdom of Solomon; and indeed a greater than Solomon is here.
>
> Luke 11:31 (NKJV)

Afterword

"Fascinating" is the word I would use to describe the process of connecting the dots of information that have emerged about the Queen of Sheba over the centuries. Scientists, historians, religious commentators, and archaeologists are among the professionals who have contributed to the wealth of available resources.

I have attempted in this novel to highlight the facts of her life through fiction, weaving throughout the storyline some of the legends which have been passed down about her.

Most likely, her reign as Queen began in Marib, then the capital of Sheba, located in the place known today as Southern Arabia. Some scholars suggest Yemen to be the precise location. Her journey from there to Jerusalem would have been over 1,400 miles.

On September 20, 2000, Mike Theodoulou contributed an article to *The Christian Science Monitor* online journal titled "Traces of the Queen of Sheba under antiquities dust." In his article, he discusses the site of the Mahram Bilqis temple near the ancient city of Marib. Radar revealed that the temple complex, half buried under the sands, "is far more extensive than was thought, making it the biggest pre-Islamic sanctuary in the Arab world...Marib was once the capital of the ancient kingdom of Saba, as Sheba was known. It is probably the richest archaeological site in Yemen…And, if the Mahram Bilqis excavation unearths Sheba's treasures, the temple could one day do for Yemen's tourism industry what the Giza pyramids have done for Egypt."

Adam Clarke in his Bible commentary writes the following about the Queen of Sheba:

"It has been long credited by the Abyssinians that this queen… was not only, instructed by Solomon in the Jewish religion, but also established it in her own empire on her return; that she had a son by Solomon named Menilek [also spelled Menelek], who succeeded her in the kingdom; and, from that time till the present they have preserved the Jewish religion."[1] (Clarke, 494–495).

According to an Ethiopian tradition, Solomon and the Queen were married.[2] There are some historians who think that Solomon did not become polygamous until later in his reign, after the Queen's visit. In the biblical narrative, Solomon's Egyptian wife was the result of an alliance with Pharaoh, king of Egypt. It is recorded in 1 Kings 3:1 soon after Solomon became King. His seven hundred wives, princesses, and three hundred concubines are mentioned in 1 Kings 11:1–4 after the visit of the Queen of Sheba. In those passages, we are told that when Solomon was old, his foreign wives turned his heart to worship other gods instead of being completely faithful to the Lord, as his father, David, had been.

At some point in time, the capital of Sheba was likely moved from Marib just across the Red Sea to Axum, located in what we know today as Ethiopia; with Menelek, the Queen of Sheba's son, becoming the first King. *The Kebra Nagast,* translated as *The Book of the Glory of Kings of Ethiopia,* purportedly contains the true history of the origin of the Solomonic line of kings in Ethiopia. "It is regarded as the ultimate authority of the conversion of the Ethiopians from the worship of the sun, moon, and stars to that of the Lord God of Israel"[3] (Budge, vii).

To add interest to this already riveting story, *The Wycliffe Historical Geography of Bible Lands* discusses that the church fathers believed the three wise men who came to adore Christ in Bethlehem were from the territories of Sheba. The gold, frankincense, and myrrh they brought as gifts were associated with the great resources of the Queen's land.[4] Isaiah 60:6 (NKJV) of the Bible is a scripture that many scholars believe applies to the birth of Jesus. It reads: "The multitude of camels shall cover your land, the dromedaries of Midian and Ephah; all those from Sheba shall come; they shall bring gold and incense, and they shall proclaim the praises of the Lord." They would have made the same journey as the Queen did.

Over 900 years later, Candace, a successor to the Queen of Sheba, awaited the return of the Ethiopian eunuch who followed the footsteps of the Queen to Jerusalem to worship. Matthew Henry wrote the following in his Bible commentary:

"We have here the story of the conversion of an Ethiopian eunuch to the faith of Christ, by whom, we have reason to think, the knowledge of Christ into that country where he lived, and that scripture fulfilled, Ethiopia shall soon stretch out her hands (one of the first of the nations) unto God. Psalm 68:31…Some think that there were remains of the knowledge of the true God in this country, ever since the Queen of Sheba's time; and probably the ancestor of this eunuch was one of her attendants, who transmitted to his posterity what he learned at Jerusalem."[5]

The story of the Queen of Sheba has been told and retold. Even today, she continues to make headlines. Dalya Alberge released in a science online publication, *The Observer*, on February 11, 2012, the article, "Archaeologists strike gold in quest to find Queen of Sheba's wealth." Here are a couple of paragraphs from it:

> Over 3,000 years ago, the ruler of Sheba, which spanned modern-day Ethiopia and Yemen, arrived in Jerusalem with vast quantities of gold to give King Solomon. Now an enormous ancient gold mine, together with the ruins of a temple and the site of a battlefield, have been discovered in her former territory.

> The idea that the ruins of Sheba's empire will once more bring life to the villages around Maikado is truly poetic and appropriate. Making the past relevant to the present is what archaeologists should be doing.

The deposits of gold in Sheba were enormous. The 120 talents of gold given to Solomon by the Queen are said to be 9,000 pounds of gold in 1 Kings 10:10 of the New Living Translation of the Bible. To give an appreciation of the value of her gift, that amount would be worth well over $150,000,000 today.

On June 21, 2012, *BBC* published an online article by Helen Briggs titled, "DNA clues to Queen of Sheba tale." The report conveyed some remarkable findings, including that "Genetic research suggest Ethiopians mixed with Egyptian, Israeli or Syrian populations about 3,000 years ago…and this fits perfectly with the story of the Queen of Sheba."

An even stranger twist to the Queen's story exists concerning the narrative of her son Menelek's visit to Jerusalem to meet his father, King Solomon. Supposedly, when Menelek returned to Sheba, he brought with him the ark of the covenant, which to this day is said to rest in a hidden location at Axum of Ethiopia in the Church of St. Mary of Zion.[6]

Some of the legends regarding the Queen of Sheba may never be proven to be true or false. But what is clear is the remarkable testimony of the Queen's life. God honors those who honor Him. During Solomon's golden years, we are clearly told that all the kings of the earth sought to visit Jerusalem and hear the wisdom God put in his heart. Yet only one written account is given us about a monarch who visited. The journey of the Queen of Sheba is the one God chose to forever immortalize in His book of truth.

What a marvel to witness God's faithfulness in showing His unfolding plan of salvation to the posterity of the people of Sheba for centuries after the Queen's death. To this day, Christians and Jews living in lands once ruled by the Queen trace the beginnings of their faith to the journey of this woman who sought to understand wisdom. Now, as she has for thousands of years, the Queen of Sheba lives on in the imaginations of people throughout the nations.

Have you not found the gospel to be in yourselves just what the Bible said it would be? Jesus said He would give you rest—have you not enjoyed the sweetest peace in Him? He said you should have joy, and comfort, and life through believing in Him—have you not received all these? Are not His ways ways of pleasantness, and His paths paths of peace? Surely you can say with the queen of Sheba, *"The half has not been told me."* I have found Christ more sweet than His servants ever said He was. I looked upon His likeness as they painted it, but it was a mere daub compared with Himself; for the King in His beauty outshines all imaginable loveliness. Surely what we have 'seen' keeps pace with, nay, far exceeds what we have 'heard.' Let us then, glorify and praise God for a Savior so precious, and so satisfying.

—Charles Spurgeon

Notes

Chapter 34

1. Psalm 72:1–4, 8–11, 15 (NKJV)

Afterword

1. Clarke, Adam. *Adam Clarke's Bible Commentary*. From the CD-ROM Version 5, *Master Christian Library*, Pgs. 494–495. Albany, OR:AGES Software, 1996.
2. Budge, E. A. Wallis, *The Kebra Nagast: The Queen of Sheba and Her Only Son Menyelek*. (Lexington, KY: Forgotten Books, 2007), 31.
3. Ibid.vii.
4. Pfeiffer, Charles F., *The Wycliffe Historical Geography of Bible Lands* (Chicago: Moody Press, 1967), 277.
5. Henry, Matthew. *Matthew Henry's Commentary on the Whole Bible*. From the CD-ROM Version 5, *Master Christian Library*. Acts 8:26-40. Albany, OR: AGES Software,1996.
6. "Aksum". *Encyclopaedia Britannica Online*. Encyclopaedia Britannica Inc., 2015. Web. 20 Jan.2015 <http://www.britannica.com/EBchecked/topic/11803/Aksum>.